Qui

Kendra pretended ignorance. "What do you mean?"

"You've been acting like a bee caught in a Mason jar, buzzing around, smacking up against the glass. Is it my fault?"

"No, it's...okay, not your fault, exactly, but..." She groaned. "Quinn, I've never been in this position before! I don't know how to be, what to do. The last time I felt this way I was a teenager."

"So was I."

"Oh." She allowed that to sink in. "Have you been celibate all that time, too?"

"No."

"Then..."

His gaze was steady. "I didn't feel like this."

"Oh." Getting hot in this kitchen. She'd almost believe she'd left the oven door open in addition to her other screw-ups. She glanced away. If she kept staring into his eyes, no telling what might happen.

A COWBOY'S CHARM

THE MCGAVIN BROTHERS

Vicki Lewis Thompson

Ocean Dance Press

A COWBOY'S CHARM
© 2018 Vicki Lewis Thompson

ISBN: 978-1-946759-45-0

Ocean Dance Press LLC
PO Box 69901
Oro Valley, AZ 85737

All Rights Reserved. No part of this book may be used or reproduced or transmitted in any form or by any means, graphic, electronic, or mechanical, including photocopying, recording, taping, or by any information storage or retrieval system, without the written permission of the publisher except in the case of brief quotations embodied in critical articles or reviews.

This is a work of fiction. Any resemblance to actual persons, living or dead, business establishments, events, or locales is entirely coincidental.

Cover art by Kristin Bryant

Visit the author's website at
VickiLewisThompson.com

Long Road Home
Lead Me Home
Feels Like Home
I Cross My Heart
Wild at Heart
The Heart Won't Lie
Cowboys and Angels
Riding High
Riding Hard
Riding Home
A Last Chance Christmas

1

Gas fumes. Which likely meant the Harley's fuel tank had sprung a leak, dammit. Quinn Sawyer had been riding enough years to be relatively confident of the diagnosis. At least Eagles Nest was less than five miles down the road, but a fuel tank leak would complicate his visit.

He'd planned on spending a couple of days with his daughter before heading back to his ranch in Spokane. A leaking tank would require extending his stay. Not a huge issue, and Roxanne always complained his trips were too short. But although she'd never admit it, having him around interrupted her graphic design work.

He had another, more immediate problem, though. Roxanne lived in an apartment over a bakery. She had no covered parking, let alone a sheltered spot where he could work on his bike. He'd personally maintained the 1983 Harley since buying it fifteen years ago. He knew her mechanical quirks and didn't trust another soul to work on her. That put him in a pickle.

The bike malfunction notwithstanding, his heart lifted as he parked in front of Pie in the

Sky and took off his helmet. Spending time with Roxanne was always a good thing. He'd solve this little inconvenience one way or another.

Every month Roxanne painted something seasonal and festive on the bakery's front window. Last month's theme had been April showers, and this month a riot of colorful wildflowers bloomed on the plate glass. The cheerful decoration and the aroma of freshly baked bread wiped out any lingering irritation over his mechanical issues.

Then Roxanne rushed out of the bakery to greet him and lit up his world. She looked so much like her mother—same long dark hair and warm brown eyes. Anne used to love wearing yellow, and Roxanne had on a shirt the color of the sun. Anne would have been so proud of the amazing woman her daughter had become.

"That's my dad! Right on time!"

"Can't keep my best girl waiting." He hugged her and stepped back. "You look great. Being in love agrees with you."

"It does." She smiled. "And you grew a mustache! What's up with that?"

He shrugged. "Something different."

"I like it. Dashing. By the way, Michael got the night off so he can have dinner with us."

"Excellent."

"Want to come in and have coffee and pie before we take your stuff upstairs?"

"That sounds terrific, but first let me check out my bike. I'm pretty sure the fuel tank's leaking."

"Yikes."

"I hope I'm wrong." He crouched down next to the Harley and inspected the tank. "But I'm not."

"Can you fix it?"

"I can, but I need a place where I can work on it."

"And wouldn't you know, I don't have one. Neither does Michael. But surely we can figure out—"

"Hey, you two!"

Quinn scrambled to his feet and almost knocked over his bike. Par for the course when Kendra McGavin showed up. That blue-eyed woman made him lose his cool. "Hey, Kendra." He also tended to smile like a goofball because she was so pretty.

She nudged back her tan Stetson. "You grew a mustache."

"Um, yeah, I did." He hadn't expected a little fringe of facial hair to attract so much attention. It wasn't like he went for a handlebar or anything.

"Looks nice."

"Thanks."

"I told him he looks dashing," Roxanne said.

"I'll go along with that evaluation." She gestured toward his Harley. "When I walked up you were studying your bike. Is something wrong?"

"Afraid so." He was mighty glad to get off the subject of his mustache. "Fuel tank's leaking."

"Whoa. That can't be good."

"It's not. I'll have to fix it before I leave."

"You intend to fix it yourself?"

"Yes, ma'am."

"Dad never lets anyone else work on his Harley." Roxanne shoved her hands in the back pockets of her jeans. "Unfortunately I don't have a garage where he can do the repairs."

"How about a vacant stall in my barn? Would that be a good location?"

Quinn gazed at Kendra. What a fascinating idea. "Yes, but—"

"Could you ride it out to my ranch?"

"Better not. It could catch on fire."

"Oh. Then let's not have you do that. Could we get it in the back of my truck?"

He shook his head. "Not easily, and even if we could, it's a dicey prospect if your truck bed isn't set up for hauling a bike. Stabilizing it would be—"

"What about a horse trailer? You could load it easier and you could tie it down."

"It works in a pinch, but I doubt you drove into town pulling a trailer."

"I could go get one."

"That's putting you to a heap of trouble."

She smiled. "Correct me if I'm wrong, but you're in a heap of trouble if you can't find a place to fix your beloved bike."

Her smile discombobulated him, but he vaguely realized there were other issues connected to this deal. "You have a point. It's just that if my bike is out at your ranch...."

"You'll be stranded there?"

"Yes, ma'am, and I have no intention of imposing on you."

"I guarantee you won't be imposing. How long do you think the repair will take?"

"If I can solder the tank to suit me, then a day or two. But I might need to locate a replacement, which could take a little longer."

"Then my ranch is your answer. I have a small cabin you can stay in and you can borrow a ranch truck when you need transportation."

"It sounds like a great solution, Dad."

He took a deep breath. "I have to admit that it does. Thank you, Kendra."

"My pleasure." She looked at Roxanne. "I'll bet you planned on having dinner with your dad tonight, though."

"I did, but—"

"Why don't you come out to the ranch for the evening? Michael, too, if he's free. Cody and Faith built a great new fire pit and I'm all about grilling these days."

"Only if you'll let us bring steaks and dessert."

"Deal. I'll be back in no time with that trailer." She hurried down the sidewalk toward her truck.

Quinn watched her go, her dark hair swinging with her brisk stride. "She's something else."

"Yep." Roxanne sounded funny, like she was trying not to laugh.

He glanced at her. "What?"

"Nothing." Her brown eyes sparkled. "See? Problem solved."

"Guess so." One problem, anyway. Staying out at Kendra's had the potential to create several more.

But even if the solution was problematic, he wanted to go. He'd been intrigued by Kendra ever since they'd met by chance at the bakery in February. Then he'd driven down in March for a Guzzling Grizzly celebration and she'd been wearing a bear suit. She sure could make him laugh.

Since then he'd traveled to Eagles Nest twice to deliver his scratchboard art to the GG because Michael had suggested displaying and selling it there. Both times he'd had lunch with Kendra and they'd had fun talking. As friends.

No doubt she'd offered her cabin and her barn in the spirit of friendship, too. But a casual lunch was one thing. Living at her place for a few days took friendship to a whole other level, one that made him a little short of breath.

No one had affected him that way in more than thirty years. He hoped to hell he wouldn't do anything stupid.

* * *

Now she'd done it. Adrenalin pumping through her system, Kendra hopped in her truck, started the engine and shifted into reverse. In the nick of time she checked her rearview mirror, saw the hood of a car behind her and shifted her foot from the gas to the brake.

Backing into someone would be damned embarrassing, especially when she'd just offered to ferry Quinn's precious motorcycle to her ranch. She still couldn't believe she'd done it, either. That's what she got for behaving like a teenager with a crush.

He'd mentioned he'd get to town around three and he'd be riding his Harley. Early on she'd figured out that the guy was punctual. Like some groupie, she'd manufactured a reason to go to the bakery at three in hopes she'd get a glimpse of him cruising in on that hog.

Easing carefully out of her parking space, she pointed the truck toward the ranch and headed home to fetch a trailer. This incident was her son Trevor's fault. Last fall he'd painted a picture of a potential sweetheart for her now that her boys had all found true love. He'd be a cowboy who'd ride into Eagles Nest on his motorcycle. And he'd have a mustache.

Now Quinn had one. On top of that, she'd gone and invited him to stay at her ranch. If she'd given herself any time to think about it, she wouldn't have. It was audacious, even for her. But when someone—specifically a broad-shouldered, Harley-riding cowboy—presented her with a problem, she hadn't been able to resist trying to solve it.

Her solution was brilliant if she did say so herself. But now she'd have Quinn Sawyer in residence for at least a couple of days. No question that he'd be a distraction, one she didn't need with Cody and Faith's wedding coming up in ten days.

Ah, but those gray eyes...

He had a way of looking at her that gave her goosebumps. She liked his salt and pepper hair, thick and touchable. And his hands. He had great hands, artistic hands as it turned out. She wouldn't mind being a fly on the wall when he created his scratchboard art. Had he brought any of his materials with him?

Quite likely not.

She respected his determination to fix his vintage bike himself. She plain respected *him*, truth be told. Fate had handed him a task very much like hers—raising a passel of kids alone after a beloved partner had died. Quinn had soldiered on, doing the job the best he could and putting his children above every other consideration.

That would have bonded them even if he hadn't been gorgeous. But he was. The visceral tug when she'd first seen him at Pie in the Sky in February had repeated itself each time they'd met. It had grabbed her again today. Exciting. Scary, too.

She drove into the clearing at the end of the graded dirt road. Wild Creek Ranch lay before her—the rambling log house where she'd grown up and where she'd raised her boys, the original hip-roofed barn and the newer, more modern one that had been built last year. The one-room log cabin that dated back to the eighteen-hundreds was partially hidden by tall pines.

Her boys plus their respective sweethearts had helped her spruce up the area in preparation for the wedding. Anything that needed painting had been taken care of. Weathered rails on the corrals had been replaced.

Pots of red geraniums sat on the porch. It was a good time for Quinn to visit.

She drove toward the newer barn and the collection of horse trailers. She could hitch up by herself if necessary, but she wouldn't mind some help.

Luck was with her. Cody emerged from the new barn and waved. She rolled down a window and called to him.

He sauntered over. "Did you talk to Abigail about the cake?"

"Not yet. Something came up." Faith and Cody had decided to forgo the traditional white frosting in favor of chocolate. Kendra had offered to deliver the request in person to Abigail, owner of Pie in the Sky. She could still do that before loading Quinn's bike.

Cody pulled out his phone. "I'll just text her. I was planning to do that anyway until you—"

"Never mind. I can mention it to her when I go back."

"Why are you going back?"

As she explained, his eyes widened. He and his brothers had asked if her lunches with Quinn constituted dating. She'd said they didn't. Now she'd invited him to the ranch. Quite likely they'd read something into that development.

Cody's expression indicated he already had. "How long will he be staying?"

"He doesn't know for sure. Depends on how the repair goes. A few days. I'd like to borrow your trailer to haul his bike, if that's okay."

"Of course. You'd better take some rope so he can tie it up good and tight, though."

"I was planning on it."

"Then let's get you hitched up."

"Thank you." She put the truck in gear and Cody guided her as she maneuvered it into position under the trailer's coupler. Then she hopped down. "I'll go fetch that rope." She retrieved it from the barn and walked back to the tailgate.

Cody had the hitch locked and was attaching the electrical connections. "I reckon you must like this guy if you've invited him to stay here."

"I like him well enough to do him this favor. He needs a place to fix his bike and we have an empty stall. And an empty cabin."

He hooked the safety chains in place and stood. "I'll toss the rope in the trailer if you want to go put on your blinkers and see if the electrical works okay."

"Thanks." She handed him the rope and went to test the connection.

"Works perfect!" Cody called out. His long strides brought him up to the cab of the truck. "Nobody's been in that cabin for a while. Want me to give it a quick airing and put some sheets and towels in there?"

"That would be great."

"You know I have to spread the word about this."

She laughed. "I can't very well keep it a secret. Oh, and I invited Roxanne and Michael to come out for a barbeque tonight. Do you and Faith want to join us?"

"Wish we could. Would be interesting. But we're due at Mandy and Zane's tonight. Mandy needs one more fitting before she's done with the wedding dress."

"Are you going to see it, then?"

"Absolutely not. Zane has some chores he needs help with at the raptor center. I won't lay eyes on that dress until our wedding day."

"That's sweet."

"I'm a sweet guy."

"Yes, you are. Well, I'd best be off." She climbed behind the wheel.

"Um, Mom?"

"What?"

"Is there any chance Quinn will stick around until the wedding? Because we could fit him in, but we'd need to know ahead of time because—"

"He won't be here that long. He has a ranch to look after and its foaling season." She smiled at her youngest son, the baby of the family. She still hadn't quite accepted that he was getting married. "He'll want to make that bike road-worthy as soon as possible so he can be on his way."

"Alrighty." Cody nudged back his hat. "It'll be weird having someone staying at the ranch who's not family."

"What about when Olivia was here for a couple of nights after the forest fire? Was that weird?"

"Well, no, but that was an emergency and she's your accountant. We know her. Besides, she's family now that she and Trevor are together."

"We put Badger up last Christmas when he came to visit Ryker."

"Yeah, but that's Badger. He's been like family from the get-go. I just mean—"

"I know what you mean." She gazed at him. "Don't worry. Quinn's simply a friend."

"A new friend."

"That, too." She put the truck in gear. "See you soon."

As she drove away, she glanced in the rearview mirror. Cody had already pulled out his phone to start alerting his brothers about this unexpected development.

Inviting Quinn to the ranch had been a spur-of-the-moment decision on her part, a minor shift in the status quo. But Cody wasn't acting like it was minor. Not surprising. He'd never seen her take an interest in a man before. But Quinn was only a friend and this visit was no big deal.

2

Quinn treated Roxanne to coffee and pastries while they waited for Kendra and chatted with Abigail and her assistant baker, Ingrid. He also bought a cherry pie and a dozen brownies to take out to the ranch for tonight's dessert. He'd almost added something for breakfast, too, but that might be overkill.

He'd positioned himself so he had a view of the street, which made it easy to spot Kendra coming back with the horse trailer. "There she is." Leaving his chair, he grabbed his jacket and put it on rather than carrying it. Then he picked up his hat. "Would you be willing to bring the pie and brownies, honeybun?"

"Sure." Roxanne stood, too. "Are you positive you don't want Michael to pop over here and help with the bike? He said he could get away if we need him."

"I appreciate that, but I can handle it. Besides, we need to do it ASAP so we don't tie up traffic for too long." He tipped his hat at Ingrid and Abigail. "Nice to see you both."

"Same here," Ingrid said. "Love the mustache."

"That's good, since it was your idea," he called over his shoulder as he held the door for his daughter.

Roxanne glanced at him as she went out. "Ingrid suggested the mustache?"

"Uh-huh." He headed for his bike. "She mentioned it in passing. I've never had one, so thought I'd try it out."

"Good impulse."

"Thank you." He waved at Kendra as she got out of her truck. She'd pulled up so the back of the trailer was even with where he'd parked the Harley. By the time he'd flipped up the kickstand and started rolling the bike away from the curb, she'd opened the back.

She let down the ramp. "There's rope in the trailer."

"Appreciate that. Nice-looking rig."

"I'll tell Cody you think so. It's his." Flashing him a smile, she turned to Roxanne. "How about putting the goodies in the truck and helping me direct traffic?"

"I'm on it."

While Kendra and Roxanne supervised traffic flow on what had become a one-lane street, Quinn concentrated on getting his bike into the trailer and securing it with the rope Kendra had brought. Then he closed and secured the trailer doors. "All set."

"Okey-doke." Kendra abandoned her post behind the trailer and hurried up to the driver's door.

He made his way quickly to where Roxanne had stationed herself at the front of the truck. "Thanks for the help." He gave her a hug, climbed in the passenger side and picked up the bakery boxes so he could sit down and close the door. "Okay, I'm buckled up." He settled the boxes in his lap. "Let's boogie."

"But slowly." Kendra stepped carefully on the gas. "I don't want that vintage bike taking a tumble."

"I tied it pretty good."

"I'm counting on that. I'm also glad that Zane graded the ranch road last week in preparation for the wedding because...well, damn."

"What's wrong?"

She sighed. "I was supposed to go in and tell Abigail about a change to the wedding cake."

"I could call Roxanne and have her tell them."

"Would you? That's why I was going to the bakery earlier. Then I saw you and forgot. I figured I'd tell her just now, but I didn't think that through. There was no time."

"I'll put the call on speaker so you can tell her yourself." He tapped Roxanne's contact number and she answered immediately.

"Dad! Is there a problem?"

"No problem. Kendra needs to relay a message to Abigail."

"Abigail's right here. I'm in the bakery."

Abigail's voice came on. "Hi, Kendra. What's up?"

"We need chocolate frosting instead of white."

"In that case, how about if I create a chocolate tooled belt around the bottom and the middle layer instead of the flowers we talked about?"

"Sounds cute. I'll have them get back to you on that. Talk to you later."

Quinn disconnected the call and glanced at her. "Hey, I feel like a jerk. I totally forgot about the wedding. It's in a week and a half, right?"

"Yes, but—"

"I shouldn't be interrupting your life at a time like this. I can just rent a truck and a trailer for my bike and drive my sorry ass back to Spokane."

"And go to all that extra trouble and expense? Don't be ridiculous."

"I'll be in the way."

"No, you won't. Cody and Faith don't want an elaborate wedding so the planning has been minimal. They're having the ceremony down by Wild Creek followed by a casual outdoor reception around the fire pit. The guest list is close friends and family only."

"That's all well and good, but you must have stuff you need to do to get ready."

"Not much, really. The Whine and Cheese Club is coming over tomorrow night to work on the favors, but other than that, we're in good shape."

"Is there anything I can do to help while I'm there?"

"How are you at filling little drawstring bags with birdseed?"

"Are those the favors?"

"Yep."

"I could do that. I'm fairly good with my hands."

She smiled. "You're hired."

"Excellent." He liked looking at her in profile. He'd sketched her from memory a few times but hadn't been satisfied with the results. After this visit he might be able to get it right.

"You can report for duty at six o'clock tomorrow night. Food and drink will be provided. But I should warn you these gatherings get rowdy."

"I don't doubt it. After seeing the five of you dancing in bear costumes at the Guzzling Grizzly celebration, nothing would surprise me."

"Don't tell them that. They'll take it as a challenge."

He laughed. "Now I'm looking forward to this favor-making gig, especially if they're not expecting me to be there. Don't say anything to them about me staying at the ranch, okay? It'll be fun to just show up unannounced."

"Are you kidding? The word's already out."

"How can the word be out? I'm not even at your ranch yet."

"Clearly you've never lived in a small town."

"Then educate me."

"It works like this. When I went back to fetch the trailer, I told Cody you'd be visiting for a few days. He was on his phone notifying his brothers the minute I drove away. Which means Zane told his wife Mandy, Mandy told her mother

Jo, who is my best friend in the Whine and Cheese Club, and Jo told the other three."

"Am I that newsworthy?"

"In a sense. People may read something into this."

"What do you mean by *this*?"

"Inviting you to come and stay at the ranch."

"So you've kept your relationships on the down-low. I respect that. And besides, it's not like we're—"

"I haven't kept my relationships on the down-low or the up-high. I haven't had relationships, period."

He stared at her. "None?"

"Nada. Zip. Zero. I haven't dated since Ian died."

"But that's been—"

"More than twenty-seven years."

"Wow. I had no idea. Have you been...okay with that?"

"Yes. I mean, for the most part, except for silly little things, like holding hands, and cuddling by the fire. I have a great life, a full life. But people may be...surprised that I invited you out to the ranch. Guaranteed there will be some gossip."

"Are you okay with that?"

"Sure."

He settled back against the seat. "Then so am I."

* * *

Less than fifteen minutes into this caper and Kendra had already revealed more about her sexual history than she'd ever intended for Quinn to know. She could have cheerfully banged her head against the steering wheel. Except she was responsible for his safety, his cherished motorcycle and Cody's trailer, so she dared not let her attention stray from the road ahead. This was the country, where wild animals could dart out in front of her and she wanted time to brake without worrying that the trailer would jackknife.

Gathering herself, she returned to the conversation. "What I'm trying to say is that there aren't many secrets in a small town. Maybe if I'd never had kids and had lived like a hermit I could guard my privacy, but those five boys I raised are woven into the social fabric of this place."

"I understand. Even though Spokane is so much bigger than Eagles Nest, my kids kept me tightly linked to the community, too. Now that all of them except Pete are determined to live somewhere else, I'm not in the loop as much."

"Eagles Nest is so small you almost can't help being in the loop. The lines of communication extend in so many different directions, especially if you've lived here all your life like I have."

"All your life, huh?"

"Born and raised in Eagles Nest. Kindergarten through twelfth grade in the school system. Graduated with three of the women in the Whine and Cheese Club. Only Jo isn't from here, but she was my neighbor for twenty years."

"I'm going to take a wild guess. Were you the homecoming queen your senior year?"

"I was, but I don't know what that has to do with—"

"Was Ian the captain of the football team?"

"Yes."

"And the homecoming king?"

"As a matter of fact. But I don't know what that has to do with the price of beans."

"I'm just trying to get my bearings. Find out if I'm messing with the town sweetheart."

"You're not messing with me, Quinn. You're a friend who's staying at my ranch while you repair your motorcycle."

"True, and you've said you're not worried about wagging tongues, but—"

"There was a time that would have bothered me." She approached the turnoff to the ranch road. "It doesn't, now."

"Good."

"My kids, though, are a different matter. I care what they think."

"Fair enough. I care what mine think, too."

"I'm glad we agree on that. But let's drop the subject for now. The road's been graded, but it's not as smooth as blacktop. I need to concentrate so I don't damage either your bike or Cody's trailer."

"I'm sure you won't."

While she waited for traffic to clear so she could make a left onto the ranch road, she glanced over at him. "Thanks for trusting me."

He smiled. "That's easy."

Her breath caught. Maybe he wasn't intentionally dazzling her. But he was doing it anyway, one smile at a time.

3

During their lunches, Kendra had talked about Wild Creek Ranch with such affection that Quinn had formed a mental picture of the place. He wasn't far off. The rambling, one-story log house with its long front porch and row of rocking chairs beckoned him to come and sit a spell.

Clearly the barns and corrals had been lovingly maintained over the years just like he'd done with his ranch. The area might have been given a facelift for the sake of the wedding, but he'd wager nothing ever looked dingy or rundown. The family had invested too much love to allow such a thing.

A young woman sat on the top rail of the round pen as a rider circled inside on a strawberry roan. A cowboy called a greeting to her before disappearing into the older, hip-roofed barn.

"It's a great place, Kendra. Not that I have to tell you that."

"It's nice to hear, all the same." She drove slowly toward the newer of the two barns. "The empty stall is in this one. Your timing is perfect. One of our boarders left for Wyoming last week and I decided to wait until after the wedding to put an ad in the paper."

"I'd be happy to pay for the use of the stall."

She flashed him a smile. "You wouldn't be trying to insult me, now, would you, Quinn?"

"Wouldn't dream of it."

"Then don't worry about paying for anything. You brought baked goods. That'll do nicely."

"Yes, ma'am."

She switched off the engine and turned to look at him. "My curiosity is killing me. What prompted you to grow a mustache?"

"Ingrid's suggestion."

"Ingrid, huh?"

"Yep. Never had one so I decided to find out if I liked it or not."

"I see." Then she murmured something that sounded like *little devil.*

"Excuse me?"

"Nothing." She looked past his shoulder. "Here comes Cody. You've met him, right?"

"I met all your sons at the Guzzling Grizzly event."

"All in a bunch, as I recall."

"Right. Which means I might not get them straight. Well, except for Bryce. I've seen him since then."

She reached for her door handle. "You'll probably have them all straight after this visit."

"I suspect I will." He'd begin with Cody. Swinging down from the truck, he strode toward Kendra's youngest.

Cody McGavin had movie star good looks in addition to the brilliant blue eyes all five sons had inherited from their mother. Quinn held out his hand and offered congratulations on the upcoming wedding.

Cody's grip was firm. Very firm. "Thank you, Mr. Sawyer. Welcome to Wild Creek Ranch."

"I'm honored to be here. And I'd be obliged if you'd call me Quinn."

Cody smiled, but his gaze was more assessing than friendly. "Yes, sir. Need some help with your bike?"

"I should be able to get it into the stall okay, but do you have any large pieces of cardboard I could put down before I roll it in there? I don't want to mess up the floor."

"I don't know if we do or not." He turned as Kendra rounded the truck. "Mom, do you have any big pieces of cardboard he can use to protect the floor of the stall?"

"Matter of fact, I do. I saved the carton my new mattress was delivered in. I'll go get it. Why don't you take Quinn up to the cabin so he can see where he'll be staying?"

"I can do that."

"Let me grab my stuff off my bike." Quinn walked to the back of the trailer and unlatched the doors. "Sweet rig you have here, Cody."

"Thanks. I bought it right before Faith and I took our big trip last summer."

"Your mom told me about that." Quinn unbuckled the bag strapped to his bike. "Sounded like a great adventure." He stepped out of the trailer and slung the bag over his shoulder.

"It was. That's a cool bike."

"I like it. You ride?"

"Not really. A buddy had one back in high school. I rode that a few times. It was fun but I wasn't willing to spend the money on one."

"Understood."

He gestured toward the hill. "Cabin's this way."

"Lead on." The dirt path could have been wide enough for two people if they were chummy, but Quinn chose to follow Cody up to the cabin. It had been well-maintained, too, but the weathered logs had been there a long time. "How old is this place?"

"As old as the ranch, so that makes it well over a hundred. First structure that went up when the land was homesteaded." Cody climbed the steps to the front porch. "My grandparents added indoor plumbing so my parents could have their own place when they got married."

"Your ancestors homesteaded this place?"

"No. My grandparents bought it from the family that did, though. By then the ranch house and barn had been built. Mom grew up here." He opened the door and walked in.

"Wow. I didn't realize that." Quinn followed him and surveyed the cozy one-room cabin.

The furnishings were simple—a double bed with a rustic headboard, a leather easy chair, a braided rug in front of the stone fireplace. The room also contained a small refrigerator, a compact stove and a kitchen sink with a cupboard mounted above it. The added-on bathroom was through a door near the kitchen sink.

Quinn put his bag on the easy chair and took off his jacket. "This is great. Like I stepped back in time." He laid his jacket over his bag.

"I know." Cody's expression had softened, as if he liked hearing that Quinn appreciated the cabin.

"And your mom and dad lived here?"

"Yep. Until my grandparents died and the ranch passed to my folks." He gestured toward the folded bedding lying on the mattress. "I brought some sheets and blankets up from the house and left the windows open so it wouldn't smell musty."

"Thank you."

"There's a woodpile out back if you decide to make a fire at night."

"Would that be okay?"

"Don't see why not. Nights are still chilly. You could use the space heaters but the fireplace is a nicer option."

"I agree. What a great setup for a guest house."

Cody looked startled. "A guest house?"

"Well, yeah. Now that nobody's living in it, having guests stay here makes perfect sense."

"I guess so. I just never thought about it that way. We don't have guests, at least not the way you're talking about. Other than when my parents lived here, it's only been my brothers using the cabin. It was Zane's place for a while, and then Ryker spent a few weeks in it after he got out of the Air Force."

"I see." He decided to hit the problem head-on. "Does it bother you that I'm going to stay here for a few nights? Am I treading on sacred ground?"

"I'd rather have you here than in the house."

Quinn laughed. "Now there's an honest answer."

He flushed. "A rude one, too. Sorry. Don't tell Mom I said that, okay?"

"Don't tell Mom you said what?" Kendra walked through the open door.

Quinn looked at Kendra. "That he'd love to take a spin on my Harley." He sent Cody an apologetic glance. "Sorry. But I wouldn't put you on that machine without letting your mother know what we're up to."

"I appreciate that, Quinn." She faced Cody. "It's not that I'm against the idea, and goodness knows you're old enough to decide for yourself. But I don't think anyone should take a motorcycle out on the road until they've had a safety course."

"That's sound advice," Quinn said. "All three of my boys took that course before they rode my bike."

Cody shrugged. "It was just an idea. Faith would likely agree with both of you and I wouldn't do it without telling her."

"And that's why I sleep better at night," Kendra said. "You might not always listen to me, but you'll listen to her and for that I'm extremely thankful." She shoved her hands in the pockets of her jeans. "Are you two ready to move that motorcycle into the barn? The cardboard's in place so I decided to come fetch you."

Quinn adjusted the fit of his hat. "Let's do it."

Kendra headed out but Cody hung back and turned to Quinn. "Thanks."

"You bet."

"Gentlemen?" Kendra called out as she stood on the path grinning, hands on her hips. "Are we doing this or lollygagging?"

"We're on our way." Quinn couldn't predict what the future would hold for him and Kendra, but unless he could get along with her sons, there was no future, period. He'd just made points with Cody. It was a beginning.

* * *

Kendra wasn't convinced they'd been talking about motorcycles when she'd arrived on the scene. But if Quinn had subtly rearranged the conversation and Cody had let him do it, then she wouldn't ask any more questions. After living with five strong male personalities for years, she'd learned not to press for specifics unless it was a life and death matter.

She'd sent them up to the cabin together as an icebreaker and evidently it had worked. They exhibited some impressive teamwork as they freed the bike from the ropes and rolled it into the barn, talking the whole time.

Kendra stayed out of the way so she didn't catch exactly what they were saying but words like *vintage* and *rare* were thrown around a bit. She smiled as Cody closed and latched the stall door. "Afraid it'll get out?"

"I don't want anyone to think they can walk in there and mess with it. It's a vintage Harley. They don't make them like that anymore."

Kendra glanced at Quinn. "I think you have a convert."

"Looks like it."

"I'll admit I'm fascinated," Cody said. "Faith will be, too. She loves old-fashioned stuff. But now that I know what that motorcycle is worth, I wouldn't dare get on it."

"That makes me very happy, son." Kendra gazed at him. "I don't care what the bike is worth but you're priceless."

He laughed. "I could take that two ways."

"Take it as a compliment. And now that the Harley's tucked in for the night, it's time to rustle up some hay flakes for our equine friends."

"I'll help," Quinn said.

"That's not necessary. You've been on the road all day and you must be tired. Zane should be here shortly and Faith will show up once she finishes with her riding student."

"I'm not the least bit tired and I want to help." He hesitated. "Unless you don't want me to."

"Hey, I never turn down free labor. We always start in the old barn because that's where we keep our favorite horses."

"Can't wait to meet them."

"And I can't wait to introduce you to them." She'd likely said the same thing to Ian the day she'd invited him to Wild Creek Ranch for the first time. Whenever she looked at Quinn, she was forty-six going on seventeen. She was enjoying the hell out of it, too.

4

Quinn wouldn't have missed feeding time for the world. Kendra was beautiful in any setting, but in that old barn, surrounded by the animals and people she loved, she glowed with happiness.

Zane arrived soon after they did. He shook Quinn's hand with a grip about as firm as Cody's had been. Handshakes telegraphed so much. "Nice to see you again, Quinn." Clearly Zane didn't feel the need to call him *Mr. Sawyer*.

Fine with him. "Same here, Zane. I surely am grateful for a safe place to fix my bike. I was up a creek without a paddle."

"Then I'm glad we had an empty stall you could use." He studied him for a moment. "Did you have a mustache last time you were in town?"

"No, that's a new addition." Back to the mustache discussion. Sheesh. His soup strainer was attracting way too much attention.

"Thought so." Zane pulled a pair of gloves from his back pocket. "Appreciate your offer to help. Use these. I'll grab another pair."

"Thanks." The worn work gloves were the same type he bought in bulk at the hardware store in Spokane. When Kendra rolled a wheelbarrow full of hay flakes through the barn door, he could almost be back at the Lazy S.

Except none of his hired hands looked like her. She'd caught her dark hair back with a silver clip at the nape of her neck and put on a pair of work gloves like the ones Zane had handed to him. She might be surrounded by guys, but she was clearly the person in charge. That stirred his blood.

She pushed the wheelbarrow in his direction about the time a horse at the far end of the barn started snorting and whinnying. "Hey, Winston! Be there in a minute, big boy!"

The horse, a butterscotch and white Paint, stuck his head over the stall door and grumbled some more.

"That's Winston Churchill," Kendra said. "Our big talker. Cody's bringing in a second wheelbarrow, so let's you and me go to the far end and work our way back. He and Zane can start from the front."

"What about me?" The same young woman who'd been perched on the rail teaching a riding lesson walked through the open barn doors. "Hey, Mr. Sawyer! I see they've put you to work already."

"My choice entirely."

"I'm Faith." She stuck out her hand. "We met before, but you might not remember."

He took off his glove and shook her hand. "I do remember. It's a pleasure, Faith. I wish you and Cody all the best."

"Thank you. I—"

"Hey, Faith!" Cody came in behind her with a loaded wheelbarrow. "You should see Quinn's 1983 Harley. You would love it."

She turned to Quinn, her green eyes wide. "You have a *vintage* bike? How cool is that! Has my dad seen it?"

"Oh, I forgot to tell you," Kendra said. "He took off early today so he could get a haircut. He was worried he'd get busy next week and forget."

Faith smiled. "He's adorable. He's afraid if his hair is a quarter of an inch too long he'll look like a hippie for the wedding." She glanced at Quinn. "I've never seen a vintage Harley."

"It's in a stall in the other barn. You're welcome to look it over when you have time."

"Cool. Thanks."

"Tell you what," Kendra said. "You and Cody can start feeding over there."

"Awesome. Thanks, Kendra." She glanced at Cody. "Off we go, bridegroom."

"As you wish, my darling bride." He lowered the wheelbarrow's handles and turned to Zane. "Over to you, bro." He hooked an arm over Faith's shoulders as they left the barn. She slipped her hand in Cody's back pocket.

Quinn gazed after them. "Cute."

"Yeah."

Something in Kendra's voice made him look at her. He caught her quickly thumbing moisture away from her eyes.

But the moment passed quickly. She grasped the handles of her wheelbarrow and started down the aisle. "Okay, Quinn, prepare to meet the Prime Minister of Wild Creek Ranch."

Kendra took time to introduce him to each horse. He met Jake, a tall bay with Tennessee Walker lineage and Strawberry, the roan he'd seen in the corral during Faith's teaching session.

Licorice was the black and very feisty mare who'd thrown Kendra, an incident that had resulted in Kendra breaking her leg. Bert and Ernie were the two geldings Faith and Cody had taken on their odyssey the previous summer.

When all the horses were fed, Quinn walked with Kendra and Zane to the new barn to help Cody and Faith finish up. Zane ended up between Quinn and Kendra on the way over. Might have been accidental. Probably not.

He looked over at Zane. "How are things going with Raptors Rise?"

"Good. The Badger Calhoun nursery is operational. Although I hate that we've had orphaned raptor chicks already, at least we have the facility for them."

"Why is it the Badger Calhoun nursery?"

"Badger donated the money for it, so I decided we should slap his name on it. I think he's pleased about it. He spends a lot of time in there. Even got himself a ghillie suit so he could feed the little buggers."

"What's a ghillie suit?"

"This thing that you put on that makes you look sort of like a large bird."

"Or a large bush," Kendra said. "Those things are a riot. But evidently they keep the babies from bonding with the humans who feed them."

"Fascinating." Quinn hadn't visited the birds of prey rescue center Zane had founded but he wanted to. "Maybe I can get over there while I'm here."

"You're welcome. Let me know in advance and I might be able to give you a tour."

"I'd like that."

"You could walk over," Kendra said. "The house where Zane and Mandy live used to belong to Mandy's mom, my best friend Jo. Jo and I, plus the kids, wore a path between the two properties."

"Or ride over," Zane said. "I've done that plenty of times."

"I'm getting the idea there's a lot of family history here." Good for him to know. Kendra was fully planted in this spot.

"Yep," Zane said. "Plenty of good memories." His voice was laced with pride and maybe a subtle warning. No interloper, aka Quinn Sawyer, was going to change things. Fortunately, he didn't have that as a goal.

Faith and Cody had almost finished distributing hay flakes, so with extra hands it was done in no time. Zane was also curious about the Harley so Quinn gave them a rundown on the bike as they gathered in the stall.

"I've had it fifteen years, got it when I was thirty-six and had teenagers in the house. Not the wisest move on my part. Timing wasn't great. They all wanted to ride it."

Faith skewered him with her green-eyed gaze. "So why didn't you wait until they were older?"

"Good question. The answer isn't very flattering. I'd always wanted a vintage bike and this became available at a price I could handle. I was surrounded by teenagers with raging hormones and issues up the gump stump. Getting on that Harley and riding away from the ranch for an hour or two was my escape."

Kendra sighed. "I can so relate."

"What're you talking about?" Cody gave her a nudge with his elbow. "We were perfect angels, right, Zane?"

"That's how I remember it. Our rooms were spotless, our homework done on time, our chores finished without complaining, our table manners—"

"I'm sorry," Kendra said, "but were you living in the same house with the rest of us? Or did you exist in some alternate universe?"

Zane smiled at her. "You don't remember it that way?"

"You know what? I don't, but I love your version. If I focus on it, I might convince myself you're right which will be such a comfort in my dotage. However, my current memory of those days is that you five were a handful and there were times I would have loved to hop on a 1983 Harley and ride off into the sunset."

Quinn chuckled. "Too bad we didn't know each other then."

"Isn't it, though?"

"But you had the Whine and Cheese Club," Cody said. "You always told us you had to get together with those ladies to preserve your sanity."

"True." Kendra nodded. "I didn't have a Harley to ride, but I had my friends. I can't complain."

"Are we making favors with them tomorrow night?" Faith asked. "I promised to let my attendants know if it was still on." Then she grinned, showing off the little gap between her front teeth that made her look like a teenager. "*My attendants.* I'm so not used to wedding talk."

"You're doing fine. And the favor-making is absolutely happening tomorrow night. Who's coming?"

"All of them—Mandy, April, Nicole and Olivia."

"And I'll be there to help," Quinn said.

The entire group except Kendra stared at him.

He shrugged. "Why not? I'll be here and I can put birdseed in little bags."

"I don't know, Quinn." Cody tugged on the brim of his hat. "That borders on unmanly behavior right there."

"I can't speak to that," Zane said. "Yesterday I helped Mandy keep this filmy material off the floor while she sewed lace on Faith's—"

"Stop!" Faith hurried over and slapped her hand against his mouth. "Do not discuss it in front of Cody." She peered at him. "You know it's a secret."

He nodded.

"If I take my hand away, will you promise not to say anything else?"

He nodded again.

"Okay, then. Don't forget. My dress is a deep, dark secret."

"It's not dark, though," Zane said. "It's—"

"Zane," Kendra said. "You'd best stop talking."

"But she doesn't want to give everyone the impression she's wearing a dark outfit to her wedding when it's actually—" He was cut off by Faith's hand smacking his mouth.

Cody cracked up. "For crying out loud, bro. Everybody knows it's not—"

"Stop talking about it!" Faith moved between them and got a firm grip on each man's ear. "Both of you."

"Ow! I was only clarifying." Cody started to free himself but glanced at his bride and evidently thought better of it.

Zane simply endured. "Sorry, Faith. I wasn't thinking. It won't happen again."

"See that it doesn't. You get to be part of the inner circle because you live with Mandy, but you'd better keep your lip zipped."

"I promise."

Quinn glanced at Kendra. "I wish I could offer you a ride into the sunset right now, but the Harley's out of commission."

"No worries. I'm told these three are scheduled to take their dog and pony show over to Mandy and Zane's house for the evening. And we need to stoke up the fire pit so it'll be ready for our steaks."

"Then let's go do that."

"Let's." Kendra smiled at her two sons and her future daughter-in-law. "See you all tomorrow, kids."

5

The kerfuffle over Faith's secret wedding dress had been nothing compared to the pitched battles that had raged when Kendra's boys had been young and rambunctious. They'd gone at it in the house, on the porch and in the yard. Mandy had often mixed it up with them, too, in those days.

Sometimes Jo had been there to help her referee, but mostly she'd handled the inevitable squabbles and misunderstandings by herself. She'd had no one in residence to commiserate with, no one to escape with.

But tonight there was Quinn, who laughed with her about the antics of her adult children because he got it. She'd forgotten how lovely it could be to have a comrade-in-arms, especially of the male variety.

Once a fire was blazing in the fire pit and beer and wine were chilling in a tub filled with ice, she asked him to help with the side dishes. Soon potatoes were wrapped in aluminum foil and tucked into the coals. A pot of ranch beans was warming on the grill.

Then Quinn earned her undying respect by offering to tear up lettuce for the salad and slice the rest of the ingredients.

"My least favorite cooking chore," she said as he stood chopping veggies on a cutting board and dumping them on top of the lettuce.

He'd removed his Stetson, but the rest of him was pure cowboy—a gray yoked shirt, tooled leather belt, worn jeans and boots that were wiped clean but scuffed, as if they'd spent plenty of time in stirrups and dusty corrals.

"Why is it your least favorite chore?" He took the jar of black olives she handed him and drained off the juice before tossing them into the mix.

"Boredom, I guess. You can't multi-task when you're making salad. The chopping seems to take forever and inevitably once I started the process the boys would come up with some crisis, or the phone would ring, or a pot would boil over."

"I've always liked making salad. You can't ruin it unless you pour the wrong dressing on top. Until that moment, your salad is perfect. Control the dressing choice and make sure it's tasty, and you have no worries."

"Uh-oh. The pressure's on. I only have one kind on hand. What if it's not the right one, at least according to you?"

"Something tells me it will be."

"You can't assume that, though. One person's yummy can be another person's yucky."

His lips twitched and his gray eyes twinkled. "I suppose."

"So much hangs on what kind of dressing is sitting in the door of my fridge." She paused dramatically, her hand on the door. "I'm almost afraid to open this and reveal what it is."

"You're gonna have to sooner or later. I'm not a fan of bare salads."

"Then here goes." She opened the door and pulled out the bottle, displaying it like a trophy. "Ta-da! Balsamic vinaigrette."

He started laughing. "Perfect."

"Is it really?" His laughter was contagious. "Or are you just saying that? Tell the truth and shame the devil."

"No, it really is perfect."

"But you're cracking up, so I'm not sure I can believe you."

He grinned. "I was going to say it was perfect no matter what you pulled out."

"Hey! No fair!"

"But I happen to really like that one."

"Seriously?"

The gleam of humor in his eyes softened to a warm glow. "Seriously."

Her breath caught. No one had looked at her that way in a long, long time. But she hadn't forgotten what that look meant. Her heart pounded.

"Hey, anybody home?"

She let out her breath in a slow sigh. She liked Michael Murphy a whole lot, but his timing sucked.

* * *

Quinn savored the moment he'd just shared with Kendra. Without his daughter's move to Eagles Nest, he wouldn't have met this fascinating woman. His life would have been the poorer for it, too.

She clearly loved to entertain. So did he, and he'd neglected that side of his personality over the years. Working with her to provide dinner for Roxanne and her fiancé was big fun.

He grilled the steaks Michael brought and sipped from a chilled bottle of beer. Other than being alone with Kendra to see where that look they'd shared might lead, he couldn't have it better than this.

When Michael went in the house with Kendra to help her bring out plates and silverware, Roxanne wandered over by the fire pit with her glass of wine. "You look right at home, Dad."

"Kendra has a great place."

"Sure does. I haven't been out here since they set up the fire pit and the picnic tables but it's a festive arrangement."

"Have you ever been inside that little cabin where I'm staying?"

"No, just seen it from a distance."

"You'd love the inside. Straight out of *Little House on the Prairie*."

"Then I should make sure I see it before you leave."

He took a sip of his beer. "I couldn't ask for a more perfect setup for fixing my bike, either. Kendra was generous to offer it."

"She's very giving. She's invited us out several times when she's having a family dinner. I guess once Michael became a partner in the Guzzling Grizzly, she considered him part of the McGavin clan. Now I'm included."

"I'll bet you enjoy that."

"I do. She always makes me feel welcome."

"That's nice." He gazed at her. "I don't have many regrets, but one is that you grew up without a mom."

"You've told me that before, but trust me, I wasn't deprived. All my friends said I had the coolest dad ever. You came to all my school events, let me have slumber parties, taught me to ride, taught me to drive, took me—"

"That's all terrific to hear, honeybun, but a girl needs her mother sometimes."

"I've heard that said, too, but anyone who believes it has never met you. I wouldn't trade you for all the mothers in the world. So there."

He smiled. "Thanks for that."

"The boys and I used to worry that you'd bring home a stepmother."

"You did? That's news to me."

"We weren't about to mention it in case we'd put ideas in your head."

"I see."

"Did you ever consider it?"

"Not really. I knew the chances of finding someone as extraordinary as your mother were slim to none. Looking for that special person would have required way too much time. Time I wanted to spend with you guys."

"See? That's what I mean. You've been the perfect parent."

He couldn't help chuckling at that. "There were days when you didn't think so."

"Oh, well." She waved a hand. "I was young and stupid."

"So was I." He glanced toward the house as Kendra and Michael came out on the porch with plates, silverware and the salad. "Bring it on down!" he called out. "Steaks are ready!" Now that it was time to dish up, he tilted his beer bottle to get the last swallow.

Roxanne lowered her voice. "So, Dad, do you think Kendra's extraordinary?"

He choked on his beer.

She took the bottle from him and pounded him on the back a few times. "Sorry!"

Kendra put the salad bowl on one of the picnic tables that circled the fire pit and hurried over. "Goodness! Are you okay?"

He nodded and kept coughing. Embarrassing as hell to have the three of them standing around watching him struggle for breath. On the other hand, although he hadn't intentionally choked, he'd been saved from answering Roxanne's question.

He knew the answer. Had probably known it from the day in the bakery when Kendra McGavin had dropped into his life. He just wasn't prepared to give it to his daughter.

She'd likely ask him again sometime. Not tonight. The opportunity for a private chat had passed. But he might want to formulate an answer so he'd be ready the next time.

Michael shared a bench with Roxanne on one side of the table and Quinn sat with Kendra on the other side. Cozy and natural as can be, and yet Quinn had never experienced having a meal with one of his kids while sitting next to a woman who was...what?

He hesitated to put a label on Kendra. Yes, she was extraordinary, but she was more than that. She was the needle in the haystack he'd never expected to find, an independent woman who unselfishly gave of herself to her family and friends. A person he could laugh with. A vibrant, exciting lady he loved talking to...and wanted to touch.

Admiration and chemistry didn't always come bundled together but this time it had. She was inches away and yet he couldn't close that gap and nestle his thigh against hers. Her warmth beckoned to him and every time she spoke, his heart beat just a little faster. In his peripheral vision, he tracked her movements as she ate her meal and drank her wine.

Meanwhile he participated in the conversation about the Guzzling Grizzly Country Store, Michael's newest project. Construction to add onto the bar's original footprint had been finished a week ago, and he was eager to see it. Customers who came in the GG's front door could choose to go left into the bar or right into the space provided for GG merchandise and signed vinyl editions of Bryce and Nicole's music.

Quinn's art would go in there, too. The store wasn't big enough to display his larger works. Those had to hang on the wall in the bar.

But Michael had requested smaller prints because the scratchboard art was selling. Evidently the clientele of the Guzzling Grizzly was the perfect fit for Quinn's depiction of horses, cowhands and wildlife.

He glanced across the table at Quinn. "You brought me some five-by-sevens and eight-by-tens, right? Because customers are already asking for them."

"I did. They're up in the cabin if you want me to fetch them."

"Tomorrow's good enough. I figured you'd want to see the store now that it's finished."

"I would." He glanced at Kendra. "If I drain the tank in the morning and solder in the afternoon, we could have lunch at the GG like we planned."

"We sure could. Roxanne, do you want to meet us there?"

"Sounds good to me. Just let me know what time."

"Excellent." Michael pushed aside his empty plate. "Any progress with the notecards?"

"Not really. I—"

"Hey, Dad. I didn't know you wanted to do notecards." Roxanne laid down her fork.

"Michael's idea. Slipped my mind, probably because I wasn't sure how to go about it."

"I can handle it for you. Just tell me which designs you want to use."

"Anything is fine. Whatever you—"

"No, wait," Michael said. "Let's do this scientifically. I can testify that horses and cowboys are the most popular. Wildlife is good but it needs to be the right wildlife. Wolves sell great. Bears do, too, obviously, because we're the Guzzling Grizzly."

"Got it." Roxanne pulled out her phone and made some notes. "Let's choose four designs. One of horses, one of cowboys with horses, one of wolves and one of bears. Is that good?"

"Works for me." Michael looked across the table at Quinn. "You okay with that?"

"Sure. I'm happy to have you two make those decisions. I'm not very objective about my work."

"Why should you be?" Kendra turned to him. "It's a labor of love. Anyone can tell that."

"They can?" That pleased him.

Roxanne nodded. "Kendra's right. You're emotionally invested in those images and it shows. People react to it."

"That tickles me."

"And now that we have that settled," Kendra said, "we have cherry pie and brownies for dessert compliments of Mr. Sawyer. Do I have any takers?"

Michael grinned. "I'll take both, especially if there's coffee to be had."

"Always." Kendra stood. "Let's get these dishes in the house before we launch into dessert mode." She glanced over at the fire pit. "Although someone needs to stay here and build up the fire."

"I'll do that." Quinn had assumed responsibility for the fire from the get-go so he might as well continue.

"Thanks." Kendra flashed him a smile. "I don't have to ask you what you want."

"Nope." He met her gaze. She was likely talking about cherry pie. But he wasn't.

6

Quinn had done such a good job with the fire that it continued to crackle merrily when Michael and Roxanne were ready to leave. After they drove away, Kendra evaluated the situation. "We have two choices. We can smother it with dirt or grab another cup of coffee and enjoy it a little longer."

"I'd vote for Option B. It's a mild night and the stars are out. But it's your ranch and your fire pit. I'll happily smother the fire if you want me to."

"If I didn't know better, I'd say you intended for this fire to last until after they left."

"Would I do that?"

"We haven't been acquainted for long, Quinn, but based on what I've seen so far, I'd say you would do that."

"Busted." He didn't look very contrite.

"Tell you what. Put on another log and I'll bring down the coffee pot. And my jacket."

"I'll move a bench over by the fire."

"Good idea, I'll be right back." Her pulse fluttered as she walked back to the house. But the prospect of sitting under a starry sky with Quinn was too delicious to pass up.

She'd meant what she'd said earlier today. She had a full life. But she hadn't experienced a night like this in ages, a night when romance drifted on the breeze and a handsome man waited by the fire.

Could she live without such things? Certainly. But when an opportunity dropped in her lap, why reject it?

Moments later she returned to the fire pit with a thermal carafe of coffee. She'd put on her denim jacket but left it unbuttoned so she wouldn't overheat in the warmth coming from the blazing logs. Or from the hot cowboy.

As promised, Quinn had brought a bench over by the fire and was sitting on it with both coffee mugs beside him. When she stepped into the firelight, he stood and picked up both mugs. "I can't remember when I've enjoyed an evening more than this one."

"I can't either." She poured their coffee and set the carafe on the end of the bench. "Perfect weather." Cradling her mug, she sat down.

"Perfect company."

"Nice of you to say."

"Nice of you to invite me." He settled on her right, leaving enough space between them for her coffee mug if she chose to put it there.

Instead she held it in both hands and took a tentative sip. "Watch out for the coffee. It's really hot."

"Just how I like it. Nothing worse than lukewarm coffee."

"Nothing?"

He chuckled. "All right, there are plenty of things worse." He took a drink before glancing at her. "You pay close attention to what people say, don't you?" Firelight shimmered in his eyes.

"I pay even closer attention to what they do."

"Smart lady."

"Like keeping the fire going even though we'd finished eating."

He shrugged. "No telling how long they would stay."

"True."

"Or whether you'd agree to sit out here with me after they left."

"Hm."

"But I was hoping."

"And here I am." Anticipation curled in her stomach.

"Nervous?"

"A little." She glanced at him. "Silly, huh?"

"Not at all." His gaze was kind. "But if you're wondering if I want to kiss you, the answer is yes. I would like that very much."

Her pulse hammered. "It's been a long time since…"

"I know. That's why it's your call."

"Then…" She took a breath and gathered her courage. "Let's try it."

Beneath his mustache, his mouth tilted up at the corners. "That's the spirit." Turning away from her, he put down his coffee. Then he reached for hers and placed it next to his.

Her breathing quickened as he shifted on the bench. Slowly, gently, as if she were a bird that might take flight, he cupped her face in both hands. "I've wanted to kiss you since that day at the bakery."

This close, she breathed in the aroma of cedar smoke clinging to his shirt. "Because I made you laugh?"

"Yeah." He stroked her cheeks with his thumbs. "And turned me on."

The tenderness of that light pressure made her shiver with delight. "I was flirting."

"I know." His gaze dropped to her mouth. "So was I."

"It's not like me to flirt."

"Or me." His grip tightened ever so slightly, bringing her closer.

"But I couldn't resist...teasing you."

"I can't resist you, period." He lowered his head, moving deliberately, giving her time to close her eyes.

She waited, heart pounding, as he brushed that smiling mouth over hers. Velvet...followed by a brief tickle when his mustache touched her lips.

When he drew back, she opened her eyes and took a shaky breath. "Is that it?"

"Thought I'd better check in." His voice was husky as he met her gaze. "Never done this with a mustache before."

She swallowed. "That makes two of us."

"How'd you like it?"

"Can't tell yet." Reaching up, she cupped the back of his head, his hair silky beneath her palm. She pulled him down until his lips almost touched hers. "Kiss me some more. And stay longer."

"Okay." He fit his mouth to hers again.

She kissed him back, taking her time. Nice. She changed the angle. That was good, too.

He lifted away a fraction. "How're we doing?"

"Not bad. More, please."

"Gladly." He returned, bringing a little more heat this time.

Wow. Potent. By the time he released her, her entire body was tingling.

"You okay?" His voice was slightly hoarse.

"Sure. You?"

"Never better." He cleared his throat.

"But I—"

"Hey, no worries. I'm a very happy man."

"You are?"

"I wasn't sure this would ever happen." He gazed at her. "What's your take on the mustache?"

"The mustache?" She blinked and touched her upper lip, which was slightly tender. "I totally forgot."

"Me, too. There's a little bit of pink above your mouth, though. I hope I didn't—"

"I'm fine." His concern made her smile. "But...we should probably call it a night."

"Good plan." He stood and picked up the coffee mugs. "Do you want—"

"No, thanks. I don't like lukewarm coffee, either." She got up from the bench.

"Then I'll toss it on the fire."

"In a highly symbolic gesture?"

He laughed. "No, ma'am." He emptied both mugs and the embers hissed in response. "That fire you lit is still burning. But it's under control. Can I walk you to your door?"

"I can't leave yet. I need to fetch the shovel so we can cover those hot coals."

"No need. I've a mind to sit out here a bit longer."

"By yourself?"

"I'm used to my own company."

"So am I."

"I sensed that about you. Makes me like you all the more." He hooked his fingers through the handles of the mugs and picked up the carafe in his other hand.

"I like you, too, Quinn." She shoved her hands in the pockets of her jacket as she walked beside him.

When they arrived on the porch, he set all three items on the porch railing. "Generally, in circumstances like this, when a man walks a lady to her door, he—"

"Kisses her goodnight?"

He grinned. "Yes, ma'am. But you still have veto power."

Damn, he was adorable. A sweet goodnight kiss sounded like the perfect ending to the evening. "Oh, what the heck?"

"I was hoping you'd feel that way." He drew her into his arms.

That's when she discovered that a standing kiss was more potent than a sitting kiss.

He tugged her in close enough to feel the coiled strength of his muscular body, not to mention the evidence of his interest in her body. When at last he ended the sensual encounter, she was gasping for breath.

He traced her upper lip with one finger. "The mustache has to go."

"What?"

"It irritates your pretty mouth. I'm shaving it off."

"That's crazy."

"No, it's not." He dropped one more light kiss on her lips and backed away. "Good night, Kendra. See you in the morning." He turned and walked down the steps, giving her a tantalizing view of his broad shoulders and tight buns.

Grabbing the mugs and carafe, she ducked inside and closed the door. Wow. Adrenaline made her light-headed as she carried everything into the kitchen, located her phone and texted Jo. *You still awake?*

The phone rang immediately. "Kendra McGavin, how dare you invite Quinn to stay at your ranch and not tell me?"

"Sorry, sorry. Everything happened so fast and I've been—"

"Canoodling with that man? Zane and Cody seem to think that something is going on between you two so naturally Mandy called me to find out what I knew, which was *nothing.*"

"Well, here's something. He kissed me."

"That's great!"

"It was great. But I'm forty-six years old and I have five grown sons. I don't know what happens next."

"Yes, you do."

"No, I don't. He's Roxanne's dad. She and Michael were here for a cookout tonight. What would she think if I got jiggy with her father?"

"I don't know. What would your boys think if you got jiggy with Roxanne's dad?"

"It would gross them out, that's what. They're not going to want to think of their mother having sex."

"Logically you've done it before. At least four times."

"Jo!" She started giggling. "You're not helping."

"Yes, I am. Instead of freaking out you're laughing."

"This is nervous laughter you're hearing. Thinking of Quinn in the abstract was kind of fun, but the reality is a little intimidating. You know how long it's been for me. I'm not sure my body remembers how to do this."

"Did you freeze up when he kissed you?"

"Well, no."

"Then I'll bet your body remembers the routine. You're both consenting adults. What's the harm in having a little fun?"

"Kissing him *was* fun."

"So what about the mustache?"

"It didn't bother me, but...hey, wait. Where did you hear about his mustache?"

"It's a hot topic around here. Does he know that one of your sons predicted you'd fall for a guy with a motorcycle and a mustache?"

"No, but Ingrid does and on his last visit she suggested he'd look good with one."

Jo laughed. "Quite the little matchmaker, isn't she?"

"Yes, she is." Kendra sighed. "I haven't decided whether to tell him about Trevor's prediction. But if the boys are thinking he grew it on purpose to fit the profile, then—"

"There has been speculation along those lines."

"Well, he did no such thing. That's not his style."

"I'm sure they'll figure that out."

"I'll make sure they do. I really didn't mean for this spur-of-the-moment invitation to turn into a big deal."

"I know, sweetie. Don't worry about what your boys will think. It's your life and Quinn is your special treat. After all this time, you deserve one."

7

Although Quinn loved every square inch of the historic log cabin, he didn't sleep particularly well. He'd stayed by the fire until the last ember winked out and stirred the ashes with an iron poker to make sure he could safely leave it.

Then he'd climbed the hill to the cabin, but not before glancing at the house to see if any lights showed. Nope. Evidently Kendra had gone to bed.

Later, as he'd tossed around on the perfectly comfortable double-bed mattress, he'd considered the possibility that Kendra wasn't sleeping, either. That would be too bad. He wanted to make her life better, not worse.

Despite a sleepless night, he'd have to say his life was infinitely better thanks to Kendra. He'd never expected to find another woman who turned him inside out. Not in this lifetime. Kendra was a one-in-a-million miracle. Consequently, his body, mind and heart were all a-twitter.

He'd lost track of how often during the night he'd glanced at his watch. Despite having a phone to tell time, he preferred a watch. He seldom wore it to bed—only when something important was happening in the morning. Like seeing Kendra again.

The watch lit up at the press of a button and he'd pressed the hell out of it until he could finally justify getting up. It was a wonder he hadn't broken the damn thing.

The bathroom was tiny but suited the purpose. He shaved, including his upper lip, and showered in a stall the size of an old-fashioned phone booth. But others had managed it and so could he.

He dressed in a clean pair of jeans and shirt, although he'd come back and change into his clothes from yesterday before working on the bike. He hadn't counted on a repair job when he'd packed for this trip. Minor issues, though, in the bigger picture.

After making his bed, he donned his jacket and hat before stepping onto the porch. A pearlescent sky and crisp mountain air greeted him. He took a deep breath, savoring the aroma from the pines that clustered around the cabin.

His property was flatter than this and not blessed with so many trees. The Lazy S was better for a breeding operation that required a lot of pasture, but not as picturesque as this. Would have been nice to have his sketchpad but he'd been traveling light.

One truck was already parked by the barn and a second one pulled in. Good. He wanted to help feed and now he wouldn't have to loiter around waiting for someone to show up and put him to work.

As he started down the hill, Zane came out of the original barn followed by Cody. They paused, glanced his way and looked at each other. Then they both responded to a greeting from the tall, lanky cowboy who climbed out of the truck that had just arrived.

The three of them gathered for a pow-wow, quite possibly about him. Maybe not, but that look between Cody and Zane had been telling. The lanky fellow was likely Faith's dad, the one who'd taken off early yesterday to get a haircut.

Only natural that the men of the ranch would keep an eye on the interloper. At least on this first morning, he'd come out the right door.

"Morning, gentlemen," he called out when he was a few yards away.

"Morning, Quinn." Zane introduced Jim Underwood, Faith's dad.

Quinn extended his hand. Everything about Jim indicated that ranching was his line of work, from the slight bow to his legs to the squint lines fanning out from the corners of his eyes. Both came from hours in the saddle.

"Pleased to meet you, Quinn." Jim met his gaze with a slight nod of acknowledgment, one seasoned cowboy to another. "Heard you had a bit of trouble with your bike."

"I did. Hoping to fix it soon. I don't want to impose on Kendra's hospitality for too long."

"Did I hear my name mentioned?"

He turned and there she was, cute as a bug with her hair pulled through the back hole of a gimme cap decorated with the Guzzling Grizzly logo. "Morning, Kendra. Great hat."

"Isn't it?" She flashed him a smile and glanced at his upper lip. Her eyes widened for a split second but she didn't allow her attention to linger. "I love my Stetson, but this makes for a fun change of pace."

"Looks great, Mom," Cody said.

"Thanks." She turned to him. "Where's your blushing bride? She's usually Johnny-on-the-spot for the morning feeding."

"Like I was telling Jim a minute ago, she's a little under the weather."

"Oh, no! That's unusual. She's one of the healthiest people I know. Should I go check on her?"

Cody shook his head. "Typical Faith, she'd rather ride it out on her own. She assured me this wasn't anything to worry about."

Quinn had to laugh at himself. He'd been so positive they'd been discussing him earlier, but more likely they'd been talking about Faith. He wasn't as important as he'd imagined. "I hope she gets better soon."

"Thanks, Quinn." Cody gave him a smile. "She does, too. She's extremely interested in that Harley repair."

Jim chuckled. "She would be. That girl loves engines of any kind."

"Hey, Quinn," Zane said. "Was I hallucinating or did you have a mustache yesterday?"

"Uh, yes, I did, as a matter of fact." Damn. He hadn't factored in how the missing mustache could be interpreted by Kendra's sons. "Turns out it was a pain. Food got in it and I had to trim it all the time. I decided it wasn't worth the effort." He avoided glancing at Kendra, but his peripheral vision told him her cheeks were pink. Her upper lip wasn't pink anymore, but women had makeup for that kind of thing.

Clearly Zane wasn't buying his lame explanation, either. "I see."

"I had a mustache several years ago," Jim said, clearly oblivious to the undertones of the conversation. "Finally concluded the same thing. Then Deidre and I got together and she made me promise never to grow one. Said she didn't relish kissing a scrub brush."

"I got the same lecture from Mandy." Zane kept his attention on Quinn. "She has extremely delicate skin so I—" He was interrupted by a loud whinny from the interior of the barn.

"Winston wants us to speed it up." Kendra started toward the barn. "I'm sure the rest of them are ready for breakfast, too. Let's get 'er done."

Bless Winston. Quinn didn't know enough about McGavin family dynamics to guess whether the conversation would have become even more pointed, but he'd rather not find out. He'd hung onto the work gloves Zane had loaned him the day before. He pulled them out of his pocket.

The group coordinated their efforts to get the feeding done. Partway through, Zane was called away to handle the rescue of a bald eagle with a broken wing. Quinn ended up paired with Kendra for the rest of the feeding routine.

When they happened to be picking up hay flakes at the wheelbarrow at the same time, he paused before grabbing the next one. He lowered his voice. "Look, I'm sorry about shaving off the mustache first thing this morning. I just wanted it gone. I didn't think about how it would look to your sons."

"It's okay. They would have had their suspicions even without that."

"But I just confirmed their suspicions."

"Oh, well." She glanced down the aisle to where Cody and Jim were working. "We'd better keep moving."

True, but he coordinated his rhythm with hers so he had another shot at conversation. "Then you're okay with them drawing conclusions about us?"

She shrugged. "So they know that we kissed. That's not such a big deal."

"Speak for yourself. I thought it was a huge deal. I barely slept last night thinking about it."

She looked shocked by the news. "You really didn't sleep?"

"Not much." He carried the hay into the next stall.

"You need your sleep," she said the next chance she had to speak to him. "You'll be working with machinery this morning."

"I'll only be draining the fuel tank. I'm not planning to solder it until this afternoon."

"Then you should take a nap before you do that."

He couldn't resist. "Only if you'll take one with me."

She flushed and her eyes darkened. "I have a riding lesson this afternoon."

"Just my luck." He gave her a wink.

"You're flirting."

"Yes, ma'am." And he'd keep doing it, too, because she liked it.

From that first meeting in the bakery, when she'd pretended to fall under the spell of a coffee drink, he'd picked up a craving she might not have acknowledged to herself. It resonated with him because he had the same craving.

They'd each lost the person they'd given themselves to, heart and soul. After that they'd virtually closed the book, figuring the story was over. What if it wasn't?

Meeting Kendra had nurtured the hope that he might find that kind of happiness again. Every time they were together, that hope grew stronger. Last night he'd kissed her and hope had transformed into something more solid, a real possibility.

What if she was his second chance and he was hers? But it wasn't that simple. He'd put down roots, building a business and raising his kids on the Lazy S. Her roots were even deeper than his. She'd spent her entire life here.

He didn't have answers. But if he kept finding opportunities to kiss her, maybe answers would come to him.

8

    Kendra and Jim had established a routine of having breakfast together at the house after the horses were fed. Zane usually headed home, but sometimes Faith and Cody would come up to eat and discuss ranch business. Or more recently, wedding plans.

    This morning, though, Cody went to check on Faith, which left Kendra with Jim and Quinn in her kitchen. She'd been relatively calm with having Quinn participate in the meal prep the night before. After sharing her kitchen with Jim most mornings for the past several months, she was used to him being there, too.

    Having them both around shouldn't have been a problem. And it wasn't for them. They had a great time discussing the pros and cons of various horse breeds, innovative training techniques and feeding regimens.

    Meanwhile they worked right alongside her to get the meal on the table. She couldn't find a single thing to complain about and yet she was on edge the entire time. She dropped an egg on the floor, forgot to turn on the coffee pot and turn off a burner on the stove.

Jim finished his meal first and pushed back his chair. "I hate to eat and run, but if you'll excuse me, I have a list of chores a mile long." He put his dishes in the dishwasher. "Nice talking with you, Quinn."

"Same here, Jim."

After he left, Quinn leaned back in his chair. "What is it?"

She pretended ignorance. "What do you mean?"

"You've been acting like a bee caught in a Mason jar, buzzing around, smacking up against the glass. Is it my fault?"

"No, it's...okay, not your fault, exactly, but..." She groaned. "Quinn, I've never been in this position before! I don't know how to be, what to do. The last time I felt this way I was a teenager."

"So was I."

"Oh." She allowed that to sink in. "Have you been celibate all that time, too?"

"No."

"Then..."

His gaze was steady. "I didn't feel like this."

"Oh." Getting hot in this kitchen. She'd almost believe she'd left the oven door open in addition to her other screw-ups. She glanced away. If she kept staring into his eyes, no telling what might happen.

"But I don't want to upset you." He covered her hand with his.

Whoa. One touch and she was plugged into a current that traveled straight to her lady parts. She took a deep breath but didn't move her hand.

His voice was gentle. "If you need me to make myself scarce, I can do that. I'd offer to leave, but that wouldn't be so easy right now."

"I don't want you to leave. Or make yourself scarce." She summoned the courage to look at him. "Not since you were a teenager, huh?"

"That's right."

"Then how come you're not, as you said, buzzing like a bee caught in a Mason jar?"

"I am. That's why I didn't sleep last night."

"But this morning at the barn you were cool as a cucumber. Just now you talked with Jim like nothing was bothering you at all. You handled the comments about mustaches and kissing without blinking."

"I don't tend to let people see what's going on inside." His thumb caressed the back of her hand.

Each slow brush across her skin ramped up the tension coiling in her body. "Is that healthy?"

"Not particularly. Read an article about it that suggested taking up a hobby as a safety valve. I chose scratchboard art."

"Wow, that's turned out well." She was surprised she could carry on a conversation considering her insides were dancing the hoochie coochie.

"It has. If I'd had a sketchpad, I could've spent the night drawing."

"So you're a self-contained man, is that it?"

"That's my default setting." He held her gaze. "Until I know I can trust someone."

"How do you know you can trust me?"

He just smiled.

The wealth of meaning in that smile sent the air whooshing out of her lungs. She was a goner. If he pulled her out of her chair right now...

Instead he gave her hand a squeeze and let go. "I'd better get started draining that fuel tank." He stood, picked up her dishes plus his and carried them to the dishwasher.

She remained seated, not sure if her legs would hold her if she tried to get up.

He returned to the table. "I'll check in with you later about our lunch plan." Leaning down, he lightly kissed her cheek. Then he left the kitchen.

After she heard the front door open and close, she flopped face down on the table, a dramatic gesture she used to do all the time at seventeen. Seemed about right.

* * *

Quinn headed up to the cabin and changed into yesterday's clothes before walking to the new barn. He'd needed the break to calm the hell down. Falling prey to RWD could be dangerous, even deadly. The acronym fit two circumstances—Repairing While Distracted and Repairing While Drunk.

He'd never worried about either one. Getting drunk didn't appeal to him anymore and over the years he'd improved on his natural ability to focus.

But the lovely Kendra McGavin was messing with his concentration. After he'd stepped inside the cabin, he'd stood immobile for at least a minute daydreaming about her. Then he'd needed another ten seconds to figure out why he'd gone up there in the first place.

Even then, changing clothes had taken twice as long because he'd ended up sitting there with one boot on and the other dangling from his hand while he relived their kitchen conversation.

She was so easy to read. She'd been born with her heart on her sleeve and that made her even more precious to him. Toward the end of that discussion, she'd been all in.

One soft word, one tender kiss, and they would have ended up back in her bedroom. She might have changed her mind after they'd arrived, especially because it was broad daylight.

He'd had no intention of making love to her this morning, though. Not that he didn't want to, but she left the ranch house unlocked and any number of people could show up looking for her. He'd forgo taking her to bed if there was any risk of embarrassing her.

Considering the number of people around the place, finding a private opportunity could turn into a major challenge. And that was assuming she let go of her reservations long enough to let it happen.

He approached the barn and stopped several yards away, cussing softly under his breath. What an idiot he was. He couldn't drain the fuel tank without a gas can and a funnel. His preoccupation with making love to Kendra had made him forget to ask her where he might find those things. No question she'd have them but he had no idea where to look.

But as he drew near the barn's open doors, the rhythmic swish and thunk of someone mucking out stalls meant he'd find help inside. Sure enough, Faith was at the far end of the barn with a wheelbarrow. He called out a greeting.

She dumped the rake into the wheelbarrow before turning toward him. "You're here!" She flipped her braid over her shoulder and started toward him.

"Yes, ma'am, but I thought you were under the weather."

"I was, but I'm fine, now." She pulled off her gloves. "You shaved off your mustache."

"I did." He waited for her comment. Everybody seemed to have one.

"Your lip, your choice. Are you going to start working on your Harley?"

Clearly she didn't want to spend time talking about his late, great soup strainer. Good. "That's the plan, but I forgot to ask about a gas can and a funnel."

"I put them in the stall already."

"Why, thank you. Much appreciated."

"I also put kitty litter in there, just to be on the safe side in case you spill some gas. I always keep it on hand. Stuff happens."

"Now I see what everybody means. You think like a mechanic."

She tucked her gloves in a back pocket of her jeans. "Dad says I started taking an interest early, around four."

"That's pretty darned young."

"Engines are so straightforward." She gave a little shrug. "Way easier to understand than people."

He laughed. "Isn't that the truth? Anyway, thanks for providing exactly what I needed. Guess I'll get started."

"Can I watch?"

"Absolutely." He walked with her to the front of the barn and opened the stall door. Besides the items she'd mentioned, a green metal tool box sat on the floor by the bike. He glanced at her. "Yours?"

"Just in case you need something you didn't bring with you."

"I'm honored that you'd share your tools."

"I don't usually." She gave him a shy look. "But that bike's in great shape for how old it is. I figure I can trust you."

"You certainly can." Crouching by the tool box, he flipped the latch, opened it and gave a low whistle. "And I thought mine was well-organized." He gazed up at her. "That's the neatest tool box I've ever seen in my life."

She gave him that cute little gap-toothed smile and her blush temporarily blotted out her freckles. "Thank you."

"Ever worked on a motorcycle before?"

"No, sir. Never had that opportunity."

"Well, you're about to."

Her green eyes lit up. "Really?"

"Might as well learn on a vintage Harley, right?"

"Heck, yeah."

Quinn proceeded to have the time of his life coaching Faith. He assisted when necessary, but mostly he talked her through the process and let her have the hands-on experience.

Along the way he fielded her questions about the engine and what he'd done over the years to keep it running smoothly. He ended up having her check out the engine, too. Working with her took longer than if he'd drained the fuel tank himself, but where was the fun in that?

They were nearly done when Cody showed up. "Thought I'd find you here. Ready to go up to the house?"

She smiled. "Quinn let me do it. Now I know how to get the fuel tank off a 1983 Harley and a whole bunch more about this bike. I think we should get one."

"And I think that's a discussion for another day."

Faith glanced at Quinn. "Translated, that means he's not on board with it. We'll negotiate."

Quinn laughed. "I know all about that. Thank you for your help with my bike."

"I had a blast. I'd love to help solder it this afternoon, but I have back-to-back riding lessons."

Cody lifted his gaze to the ceiling. "Thank you, God."

She gave him a mock glare. "Quinn would be there and he knows exactly what he's doing."

"I'm sure he does, but..." He glanced at Quinn. "Nothing against you, sir, but we're—"

"Getting married a week from Saturday." Faith completed Cody's sentence. "And you want to make sure I don't catch my hair on fire. I get it." She turned to Quinn. "Thank you so much. Keep the tool box until you're finished."

Cody glanced at it in obvious surprise. "You loaned him your tools?"

"Yes, I did."

"Hey, Quinn, you rate, buddy. She guards those with her life. I count myself privileged because she lets me use them if I ask her first."

"I count myself privileged, too. Thanks, Faith."

"You're welcome." She looped her arm through Cody's. "See you tonight, Quinn."

He drew a blank. "Tonight?"

"When we're making favors. You said you'd be available."

"Which I most certainly will be. Wouldn't miss it." Especially now that he knew the bride a lot better. He was a little sad he wouldn't be here for the wedding.

But his life was in Spokane. Most of it, anyway. He couldn't deny that a tender sprout had taken root in Eagles Nest.

9

Kendra had the checkbook open and was paying bills when Jim came into her office. She glanced up in surprise. "Hey, there. What's up?"

"You tell me. Cody sent me a text asking if I'd meet him here. He hasn't arrived yet?"

"Haven't seen hide nor hair of that boy. And he didn't mention wanting to have a meeting this morning. I suppose it could be about the new fencing he's had his eye on." She gestured to one of the two chairs in front of her desk. "Have a seat. I'm sure he'll be along any minute."

"No doubt." Jim settled into a chair and laid his hat on his knee.

"Nice haircut."

"Thank you kindly. Deidre thinks it's too short, but this is how I like it."

"And it's your hair, not hers."

"Exactly what I said. I don't tell her not to color hers every shade in the rainbow, now, do I?"

Kendra laughed. "A wise man would never try that and I know you're a wise man."

"I told her we didn't need to be discussing our hair, meaning I wouldn't discuss hers if she would stop complaining about mine."

"Did that work?"

"Not really. Doesn't matter. I love her and that's that. She makes my life more interesting."

"She makes everyone's life more interesting. I can't imagine what I'd do without her."

"That makes two of us. Just the other day, she—" He glanced toward the door. "And here's Cody and Faith. What a nice surprise. How're you feeling, sweetheart?"

"Much better, Dad. Thanks."

"That's good to hear," Kendra said. "I was wondering if I needed to come up there with a pot of chicken soup."

"No need, but thank you for thinking of me." Her cheeks turned pink.

Strange. Chicken soup wasn't exactly a delicate subject. "Well, come and sit down, at any rate. Sorry, Cody. We're out of chairs. You'll have to hold up the wall."

"No worries." Instead of leaning against the wall, his usual behavior when the chairs were all taken, he came to stand behind Faith's chair. He rested his hands on her shoulders. "We won't be here long." His eyes sparkled like they did when he had good news to share. "We wanted to tell you this together, since—"

"Oh, my God!" She leaped to her feet as the pieces fit together—Faith's mysterious ailment that had apparently disappeared, her blush a moment ago and this meeting where Jim had to be present. "You're pregnant!"

"Yes." Cody's smile was a mile wide. "We're going to have a baby. Which means you two—"

"Are going to be grandparents!" With tears in her eyes, Kendra rounded the desk to start the hugging.

She began with Cody while Faith jumped up and hugged her dad. Then Kendra moved on to Faith and finished up with Jim. She'd never been quite that familiar with Jim before, but it seemed appropriate since they were going to be grandma and grandpa to this baby.

"This is so exciting." Kendra glanced at Jim, who looked shell-shocked. "Isn't this exciting, Jim?"

"Sure is. I never imagined...well, of course, since you two are getting married, I figured eventually, but I—"

"We jumped the gun," Faith said. "Once we set the wedding date, we decided what the heck, why bother with birth control? We want kids but thought it would take a while. Turns out it didn't."

"It certainly didn't." Cody looked inordinately proud of himself.

Kendra was blindsided by a flashback. Ian's expression had been exactly like that when she'd discovered she was pregnant with Ryker. Like he deserved a medal or something.

She was torn between laughter and tears. She ended up with a messy combination of both.

Cody gathered her close. "You're gonna be an awesome grandma."

"You bet I am." She sniffed and backed away. "Got a bandanna for grandma?"

He chuckled, pulled one out of his hip pocket and gave it to her.

She blew her nose and handed it back to him with a watery grin. Returning a used bandanna was an old joke they shared.

He laughed and tucked it in his pocket. "I suppose you'll teach baby whozit that trick."

"Of course." She gazed at him. So young, yet so confident. She had been, too. "When can we expect this bundle of joy?"

Faith's eyes shone with happiness. "Mid-December."

"A Christmas baby! That's perfect. You two will be such good parents."

"I hope so," Faith said. "But we're counting on you and Dad as backup. I don't know anything about babies and Cody doesn't, either. He *was* the baby, whereas the other boys remember taking care of him."

"Don't worry," Kendra said. "We've got you covered. Right, Jim?"

"Right." Jim looked a little wobbly. If it hadn't been eleven in the morning, she would have suggested they have a drink to toast this kid, Faith abstaining, of course. "Are we the first to know?"

"Doc Pulaski is technically the first to know," Cody said, "but she's a vault. She won't squeal until we tell her the word's out."

"And when will that be?"

Cody pulled out his phone. "As soon as I text my brothers."

"You're going to *text* them to say they're going to become uncles?" She was horrified.

"Sure, why not? It's the most efficient and democratic."

"You need to tell them in person!"

"Not practical. We could control how we announced it to you two, but it could take me all day to track down my brothers. Besides, I'll have to start with someone, and I guarantee before I made it over to the next one, word would somehow spread and the rest would already know and be upset because they weren't my go-to."

"I see your point."

"I composed the text first thing this morning." He hesitated. "But once I send it, all hell will break lose. Faith left her phone up at our place and we'll head up there, because guaranteed we'll be on the phone for a while. Is there anything else we need to discuss among ourselves before I pull the trigger?"

"Yes!" Kendra clapped her hands together. "We should celebrate. Let's do a family dinner. How about tonight?"

"Can't," Faith said. "We have the favors to make tonight with my attendants and the Whine and Cheese Club."

"Oh, right. Then tomorrow night."

Cody shook his head. "It'll be Friday night at the GG. Bryce and Nicole usually do a number at intermission. Same on Saturday night."

"Do you know if Nicole is doing her solo gig on Sunday night?"

"Maybe not. They've been trying out some new musical groups to buy her some free time on the weekend. Sunday night could work."

"I'll find out." She glanced at Jim. "I know you'll want to tell Deidre, but if you don't mind, I'd like to break the news to her."

"Yes, ma'am. You have the prior claim, growing up with her and all."

"Better get prepared with a group text, then, Mom." Cody winked at her.

"You can text if you want. I plan to call."

"Are you sure about that? As soon as Zane reads the one I'm about to send, he'll tell Mandy, who will tell Jo, who will tell—"

"Okay, okay! I'll text!" She grabbed her phone off the desk. "Do I have time to add a dancing baby?"

"Sure." Cody lounged against the edge of the desk. "I'll wait."

She typed in the message and glanced up from her phone. "I'm all set. Send yours. I'll wait two minutes and send mine."

He looked over at her desk. "Anything urgent that you have to finish before lunch? Because I guarantee you won't get anything more done this morning once we send these texts."

"Nothing's critical. Oh! I didn't even think to ask. Do you know yet if you're having a boy or girl? I've heard you don't have to wait long these days to find out."

"We decided we didn't want to know," Faith said. "We told Doc Pulaski and she promised not to tell us."

Jim nodded. "Good decision. Nothing wrong with a little suspense. Makes the outcome more exciting."

"I agree, Jim. I'm going to add that info to my text." She typed it in. "Saves people asking."

"Then are we all good here?" Cody held up his phone. "Once this starts ringing, Faith and I will vamoose. I don't want to turn the office into a call center."

"I'm ready." Kendra met his gaze. "Do you feel like the guy at the race holding the starter pistol?"

"I kinda do. Doc Pulaski said something that's stuck with me—*Your life has changed and it'll never change back.*"

Kendra smiled. "But the best part is, you won't want it to."

<u>10</u>

Now that Quinn had examined the fuel tank, he doubted that soldering it would fix the problem. He'd give it a shot after lunch, but he wasn't confident about the outcome.

Because of that, he'd left several messages with friends he'd made in the fifteen years he'd been riding the bike. The network of Harley owners was large and dedicated to helping fellow riders. Someone was sure to have a lead on a replacement tank in this area.

He was washing up in the miniscule cabin bathroom when Kendra's text came in with a suggested time to leave for town. He responded that he'd be ready.

I have exciting news, she texted back. *And Ryker's joining us for lunch.*

Great! He's your oldest, right?

Right. Will you please text Roxanne?

Sure.

He sent Roxanne a message advising her to give them extra time for a tour of the store before she showed up. No point in interrupting her work any longer than necessary.

Then he set down his phone and finished changing into the clothes he'd worn this morning. He wasn't the least bit surprised Ryker was joining them for lunch. In fact, the guy was showing up later than Quinn would have expected.

Besides being the oldest, Ryker was an Air Force vet. He likely had a protective streak a mile wide when it came to his mom. Quinn was about to be scrutinized.

Fine with him. He took the matted five-by-seven and eight-by-ten prints out of his bag. He'd created small-scale originals and made prints of those instead of using his larger works. The format had been a good change of pace.

He'd wrapped each one individually and then bundled them all together into one neat package that had been easy to transport. Putting on his hat, he picked up the parcel and left the cabin. Showtime.

On the way to the house he saw Jim down by the new barn and gave him a wave. Jim waved back before disappearing through the double doors.

Quinn figured he'd made a friend, especially if Faith had mentioned anything about working on the Harley. He'd bet Jim was as fiercely proud of Faith as Quinn was of Roxanne.

A muscular black truck was parked near the house. Ryker's, no doubt.

Quinn's boot heels tapped against the flagstone-paved walk as he headed for the front porch. The fire pit and picnic tables were off to his left and he gave them a fond glance before climbing the steps. Wild Creek Ranch was growing on him.

Pausing at the front door, he rapped on it. "Come on in!"

Kendra's cheery greeting jacked up his pulse rate. She sounded excited. Happy. He opened the door, expecting Ryker to be inside with her.

But the living room was empty and she was alone when she came out of the kitchen drying her hands on a towel. Her cheeks were flushed. "I have the best news. Faith and Cody are having a baby!"

"Kendra, that's wonderful!" He put down his parcel on the nearest surface, crossed the room and pulled her into a hug. Then he let her go just as quickly and glanced around. "Sorry. Wasn't thinking. Where's Ryker?"

"He walked up to Cody and Faith's house to congratulate them in person. He should be back any minute. Let me get rid of this towel. I was starting the prep work for tonight's party."

He followed her into the kitchen. *Any minute* meant he'd better keep his hands to himself. He shoved them in his pockets. "So when's this bundle of joy due?"

"Middle of December." She combed her hair back with her fingers. She'd taken it out of the ponytail and had likely worked some magic with a curling iron. "There was something else I needed to tell you, but this baby news has me all flustered. I can't remember what it was."

"It'll come to you." He itched to touch her. "Your hair looks nice."

"Thanks. I wanted to...well, it doesn't matter. Anyway, there'll be a little McGavin around during the holidays. That hasn't been the case for more than twenty-five years."

"Should be fun. You'll be a—"

"I know. Grandma Kendra. Can you believe it?"

"No, frankly, I can't. Nobody who looks at you will believe it, either."

"I'm thrilled about this baby. Over the moon. But..."

"Not quite ready for the designation?"

"No! I realize grandmothers are running marathons and heading up multinational companies and sometimes are only forty-six. I've been telling myself that this new status doesn't change anything. I'm the same person. On the other hand, it changes *everything.*"

He nodded. "I get it. I haven't faced this yet, and I'm sure I'll be excited when—and if—it happens. It throws you into a new role, though, one you might not have envisioned for yourself quite yet."

"So true, and I wasn't prepared. Which is unrealistic because my kids are older than I was when I had them, for crying out loud."

"Mine, too, come to think of it." That was sobering. Considering the age of his kids, he was past due to become Grandpa Quinn. He wasn't ready, either.

"None of my girlfriends expect to be grandmothers any time soon. I'll be the first and let me tell you, the whole concept feels just plain *weird.*" Then she clapped a hand over her mouth and her eyes widened.

"It's okay." He smiled. "I won't tell anyone you said that."

"Thank you. I can't believe I did. But I do feel weird and I've been coming up with wild ideas, like maybe I should buy a sports car. And color my hair."

"I can see you zipping around in a sports car."

She laughed. "Totally impractical, not to mention expensive, so I won't do it. But I might pay a visit to Nicole at Shear Delight and see what she—"

"*Please* don't."

She gave him a puzzled look. "You sound passionate about it."

"I am. The silver in your hair is like…starlight."

She blinked. "I hardly think so."

"I doubt you're in a position to judge, especially today, but take my word for it. Those little hints of silver in your dark hair are mesmerizing."

The corners of her mouth turned up.

"You don't believe me."

"No, but I'm enjoying the heck out of the conversation."

"Promise me you won't color your hair."

"I won't make that promise, but I will promise not to be hasty about it. How's that?"

"Better. If you get the urge to make that hair appointment, call me. I'll stage an intervention."

She laughed. "You're so good for my ego."

"Glad to hear it. You're good for mine, too."

"I've never once complimented your hair, although I think it's very nice."

"I don't give a damn what you think of my hair. But I love it when you look at me the way you did this morning."

Color bloomed on her cheeks. "I can't imagine what you're talking about."

"You know very well what I'm talking about." He lowered his voice in case Ryker suddenly walked into the house. "The heat in your eyes nearly set this kitchen on fire. If I hadn't been worried about someone walking in on us, I would've done something about it."

She sucked in a breath. "Quinn Sawyer, the things you say."

"Still feeling grandmotherly?"

"Not even slightly, you crazy cowboy."

"Crazy about you."

The front door opened. "Hey, Mom, is Quinn here yet?"

"Sure am." He gave Kendra a wink before turning and walking into the living room. "Good to see you again, Ryker."

"Same here." He smiled, but like his brothers, his handshake was a hair shy of being painful. "Sorry about your bike."

Quinn wasn't sorry. Delighted, in fact. But he played along. "Yeah, tough break. Not surprising, though. My first long ride since last fall."

"Faith raved about that Harley. She wants one."

Kendra came out of the kitchen. "That wouldn't make much sense now that they're having a baby."

"I think she knows that," Ryker said. "But I wouldn't put it past her to get one eventually now that she's had a chance to work on Quinn's."

"Work on it?" Her eyebrows lifted as she turned her attention to Quinn. "Didn't Roxanne say you won't let anyone work on it besides you?"

"Normally I don't, but then Faith brought me her extremely neat tool box and offered to let me use anything I needed. She doesn't usually loan out her tools, either."

She smiled. "You found a kindred spirit."

"Matter of fact." He was in danger of being drawn in by the soft glow in her eyes so he looked away. "Who's ready for a burger at the GG?"

"I'm always up for that," Ryker said. "We taking the van?"

Kendra nodded. "Probably should since there are three of us. Quinn, did you bring your artwork?"

"Sure did." He walked over to the side table where he'd put it down. "Right here."

"Then let's go," Ryker said. "I'll drive."

"Thank you for the offer." Kendra picked up her keys and a small purse dangling from a hook by the door. "But I enjoy driving that van."

Ryker folded immediately. "Okay."

Quinn loved it. Her boys might tower over her and outweigh her by at least a hundred pounds, but she held her own with that crew. He lost another chunk of his heart to Kendra McGavin.

When Ryker made a beeline for the driver's door to open it for his mother, Quinn readily surrendered the privilege. Ryker also offered up the co-pilot's seat, but Quinn let Ryker have it.

Climbing in behind Kendra's seat, Quinn buckled up and initiated a conversation with her eldest son as she fired up the engine. "Air Force, right?"

"Yes, sir. Flew F-15s. Did you serve?"

"Army. Armored division."

"How many years?"

"Four. Married my high school sweetheart when I was on leave and we started having kids right away, so I didn't want to stay in."

"Makes sense."

"How about you?"

"Ten years." He grimaced. "And my high school sweetheart and I broke up when I enlisted. Lucky for me, April's taken me back."

"And we're all fortunate that she did," Kendra said. "April's a sweetie."

"No question about it." Ryker's chiseled features softened. "I'm a lucky guy."

"I don't think I've met April. Is she coming to lunch?"

"Unfortunately not. She would have, but she agreed to a couple of last-minute massage appointments that wiped out her lunch break. When people are hurting, she hates to turn them away. Badger's coming, though."

"*That's* what I forgot to tell you," Kendra said. "He thinks your scratchboard art is really cool so he asked if he could have lunch with us today."

"Great." Quinn turned to Ryker. "Am I right that he's the other half of Badger Air?"

Ryker nodded. "That's him."

"I definitely met him at the event in March." He grinned. "Badger makes an impression."

"He's become one of the family," Kendra said. "He's only been around since Christmas but now I can't imagine how we got along without him."

"He can't imagine how he got along without us, either." Ryker glanced at Quinn and his blue eyes flashed a subtle warning. "He thinks my mom hung the moon."

Quinn met his gaze. "I have it on good authority that she did." Lunch would be interesting.

11

Kendra admired Quinn's diplomacy. He'd given up the front seat to her son and zeroed in on Badger Air as a promising conversational topic. He'd correctly guessed that Ryker would enjoy talking about his beloved airline, his passion for flying and his close friendship with Badger. Her eldest had loosened up.

For the most part it was guy talk and she tuned out most of it. Having lunch with Badger today would be fun. She hadn't crossed paths with that sweet guy in a week or more and she was eager to get her Badger fix. If he wanted to rave about Quinn's art, so much the better.

Ryker's primary motivation for going to lunch had nothing to do with Quinn's art. His protective instincts were on alert. When she'd insisted that Quinn was only a friend and his visit wouldn't lead to a major change in the status quo, Ryker hadn't bought it.

He wasn't a fan of change. Despite causing a seismic shift when he'd virtually abandoned the ranch ten years ago to serve in the Air Force, he'd expected both the ranch and Eagles Nest to be the same when he'd returned. Kendra had pointed out the contradiction several times, but Ryker wasn't ready to acknowledge it.

Fortunately for him, the ranch itself hadn't changed much other than the new barn. He and his brothers had altered their status from singlehood to committed relationships, but that was a logical progression.

Eagles Nest wasn't given to rapid change, either. The residents worked hard to preserve the historic character and friendly atmosphere of the place.

As Kendra approached town, Main Street looked about the same as it had when she'd been a child here. Old-fashioned street lamps lined the thoroughfare as they had for more than a hundred years. Many of the original buildings and businesses remained, including the Guzzling Grizzly, although it had recently been enlarged to accommodate the GG Country Store.

Ryker wouldn't dare complain about that change. Two of his brothers had been heavily involved—Bryce as co-owner of the GG and Trevor as an employee of the construction company that had built the addition.

But everyone connected with the project had focused on making the store blend with the existing structure so it didn't look like an afterthought. Preserving the GG's standing as a familiar Eagles Nest landmark had been a top priority.

Kendra was as much in favor of stability and familiarity as anyone. Ryker might be concerned that Quinn was a threat to the family dynamic they all cherished, but she wouldn't allow that to be disrupted. Quinn didn't seem like the type of person to do that, anyway.

Well, unless she counted the turmoil he'd created by kissing her. Or the havoc he'd played on her senses this morning at breakfast and again just recently with a few suggestive words.

But that was a private matter, something that didn't have to touch her sons' lives at all. Jo had told her she deserved this after all the years of putting her children first. Now that she was about to become a grandmother, she was inclined to go along with what Jo recommended.

A grandmother. The designation didn't compute. Not that long ago she'd been a young bride, then a young mother. Sure, her boys had become men, but she hadn't changed that much. And Quinn thought the silver in her hair looked like starlight.

The GG parking lot was crowded but she found a space. She never minded having to search for a spot because that meant the Guzzling Grizzly was prospering.

Ryker got her door for her and Quinn didn't compete for the privilege. Clearly he wasn't interested in making waves. *Just making love.*

With a spring in her step, flanked by Quinn and Ryker, she started toward the front door.

"The addition looks terrific," Quinn said. "You'd think it had been here all along."

"That's what they were going for." Ryker got to the door first and held it for them. "Are we heading for a table first or the store?"

"The store," Kendra said. "My guess is that Bryce will be in there."

"And I can drop off my artwork."

"That, too. I can't wait for you to see how the place turned out." She led the way through an arched entrance to the right.

As usual whenever she walked in, the shop was busy. Bryce and Michael had hired one of Cody's high school friends, Katie Greer, to work the register. After only a week, the store was making more than enough to pay her.

Kendra moved aside so Quinn could get a better look at the interior.

He glanced around and let out a low whistle. "This is incredible."

"Isn't it?" She beamed with pride. "Bryce, Michael and Trevor spent hours planning this. Rough paneled walls were a given, but they wanted the shelving to look old, too, so they searched for old barn wood. The oak barrels—"

"There you are." Bryce walked up behind them. "I had to check something in the kitchen and didn't see you come in. Hey, Quinn."

Quinn turned and they shook hands. "Impressive setup."

"Thanks."

"If you'd told me this was here a hundred years ago, I'd believe you. Even the floor looks old."

"It is, and it gave us fits. Zane located the planks. He was up in Helena checking on a new regulation that might affect his raptor rescue and spotted an old warehouse slated for demolition. We got the wood for a song, but—"

Quinn chuckled. "You performed for them?"

"No, but I would've if they'd asked. That's how bad we wanted those planks. Except they're slightly warped. Greg Paladin and his crew planed and sanded for hours to create a floor that wouldn't trip the customers."

"And looks like it's been here forever," Kendra said. "Show him the pot-bellied stove Badger and Ryker hauled from Kalispell in the Beechcraft."

Quinn glanced over at Ryker. "That must have been a trick."

"One of the heaviest, messiest passengers we've ever had. Quiet, though."

"And it's a beauty." Bryce led them over to a far corner. A black cast iron stove sent out a cheerful glow. Two ladder-back chairs and a small table were positioned near it, along with a checkerboard.

Quinn walked closer to the stove and laid his hand on it. "If this is a replica, it's a damned good one. They've even added nicks and scratches."

"It came out of an abandoned line shack," Ryker said. "April and I saw it in an antique shop when we were up there visiting her folks. Badger helped me wrestle it onto the plane."

"Then Faith installed the electric heater." Bryce crouched down and adjusted a control underneath the stove. "Much as I would have loved a real fire, it's too much of a liability."

"I sure do like what you've done here," Quinn said. "Sounds like the whole family got involved in creating this place."

Bryce nodded. "Pretty much. Nicole and Mandy decided on the traffic pattern for the aisles and added some decorative touches like the lariats and bandannas."

"Even Cody did his part," Kendra said. "He talked Katie into applying for this job instead of taking one in Bozeman. The only family member who didn't contribute something was me."

And that was the way it should be. She'd been a cheerleader for this project but she'd watched from the sidelines. They'd accomplished it completely on their own. She took great satisfaction in that.

"Wrong, Mom." Bryce wrapped an arm around her shoulders. "You made a huge contribution. Without you, we wouldn't be here."

"Well, there's that, I suppose, but I wasn't asking you to reassure me that I'm appreciated. I know I am, but I'm tickled pink that you were able to pull it off without me."

Bryce looked confused. "You are?"

"I sure am. It's a parent's duty to work themselves out of a job." And snip, snip, a couple of apron strings fell away. She turned to Quinn. "Don't you agree?"

He was watching her with a gleam in his gray eyes. "Absolutely."

"Um, yeah, that makes sense, I guess." Bryce exchanged a glance with Ryker.

Kendra was fascinated by the effect of her little speech. Neither of her boys seemed particularly happy about it. Quinn was, though.

She would love to get his take on the dynamic. But that would require privacy and they wouldn't be getting any of that soon. Maybe not until tonight, after the favor-making party broke up.

And then what? She was confident now, but would she hold onto her bold attitude once she was alone with Quinn? Or would she be all hat and no cattle?

* * *

Quinn silently cheered Kendra's personal declaration of independence. Her boys weren't crazy about it, though.

Bryce seemed eager to change the subject. He turned to Quinn. "Looks like you brought the artwork we talked about. How many prints do you have?"

"Six." He handed over the parcel. "Thought that was plenty to start with until we see how they sell."

"I guarantee they'll sell." Bryce started unwrapping the package. "Customers have been asking for these. Something they can tuck in a carry-on bag."

"I hope they work out, but you don't have to unwrap them now. I'm sure everyone's hungry."

Kendra moved closer to Bryce. "I'm not starving and I want to see them."

"Me, too," Ryker said. "Take them over to the counter where you can spread them out."

"Sure. Good idea."

A few customers caught on to what was happening and gathered around Bryce as he began laying out Quinn's work.

Quinn edged away from the crowd. He'd rather go sit at the bar and order a drink, but that would be antisocial.

Although he thoroughly enjoyed making his art, he truly hated being there the first time anyone looked at it unless it was his kids. They could be counted on to react positively. Other folks, not so much.

Kendra put a hand on his arm. "What's wrong?"

He kept his voice down. "I'm not fond of this part."

"What part?"

"Having people comment on my art."

"Even if they say good things?"

"Even then. And mostly they do. But it's just..." He massaged the back of his neck.

"You put yourself into it, your private self."

"I do." The warm understanding in her eyes helped. "And I feel exposed when I show it to anyone except my kids. But Roxanne convinced me I need to share."

"She's right about that."

"Making money's not so bad, either. I never expected to do that and in the horse business you can always use a little extra. So I—"

"Hey, Quinn," Bryce called over his shoulder. "These are perfect. Just what people are looking for. You have customers already."

"Excellent." He glanced at Kendra. "You wanted to see. Go ahead."

"I do. I just didn't realize what you go through."

"It's okay." He smiled. "Go look."

"All right."

He followed her over to the counter. Yeah, he was nervous. She'd complimented his larger pieces hanging in the bar, but at the time he hadn't known her well enough to tell the difference between courtesy and genuine appreciation.

His gut tightened as one of the customers moved aside to give her room. Her quick intake of breath was followed by a sigh of pleasure. She wasn't capable of faking a reaction like that just to be polite. She liked his art. A lot. And that, he'd just discovered, mattered.

That hurdle behind him, Quinn was more than ready for a burger and a beer. As he left the store with Ryker and Kendra, Badger walked through the door of the GG.

After giving Kendra a hug and carrying on about the baby announcement, he turned to Quinn. "Hope you don't mind me crashin' the party, but after Cowboy said he was havin' lunch with y'all, I invited myself."

"Cowboy?"

"That's the handle I got in the military," Ryker said.

"And it stuck to him like Badger stuck to me."

Quinn smiled. "Got it."

"Anyway, I horned in on this gathering because I'm plum fascinated by your scratchboard art. I'd like to give it a try."

"Do you draw?"

"Yes, sir, at least I used to. About the only class I enjoyed in college. Then I enlisted and let the drawin' go by the wayside. The scratchboard concept appeals to me. I figured you could steer me in the right direction."

"Glad to. I—"

"Hi, everybody!" Roxanne came through the door and fussed over Kendra before glancing at him. "Dad! You shaved off your mustache!"

"Sure did." Damn, he should have mentioned it in his text earlier and asked her to soft-pedal her response.

Ryker frowned. "What mustache?"

"When he got to town yesterday afternoon he had one. I thought he looked really good, too. Wasn't that your first ever, Dad?"

"Yes, but I—"

"I can't believe you shaved it off already." She glanced at Kendra. "You agreed it was dashing, right?"

"I did."

Quinn didn't have to look at Kendra to be positive she was blushing. Time to defuse the situation. "To tell the truth, honeybun, I'm so naturally handsome that the mustache was overkill, so I ditched it. Let's go eat."

Kendra's little snort of laughter was music to his ears.

<u>12</u>

Kendra was still smiling about Quinn's comeback as she took a seat between Quinn and Ryker at one of the round tables that had recently been added to the mix. Badger claimed the seat on the other side of Quinn and Roxanne sat next to Ryker. The tables could accommodate six, so pushing two four-tops together wasn't necessary anymore unless all the round tables were taken.

Subtle adjustments like that were one of Michael Murphy's strengths. After they'd settled in, he came out from behind the bar and crossed the room to their table. "So, Quinn, what do you think of our..." He paused. "Didn't you have a mustache last night?"

"That's what I just heard, too," Ryker said, "but now it's AWOL. He said—"

"Hey." Kendra held up both hands. "Enough on this topic, okay? He had one yesterday but he doesn't have one today. End of story. Let's drop the subject of mustaches."

"Let's not." Trevor appeared behind Michael.

Badger grinned. "I had no idea this party would get so entertainin'. Have a seat, Trev."

"Thanks, but I can't stay. My lunch break isn't long enough. I—"

"Trevor, I'm so glad you're here." Kendra pushed back her chair. "I'm having a little issue with the supports for the chicken coop. But I don't want to bore everyone with it. Let's go talk over by the bar so I can fill you in."

"Uh, sure." Trevor followed her to the bar. Once they were out of range of the table, he started in. "If that guy grew a mustache just so he could fit the—"

"He didn't, so cool it, son. He doesn't know anything about that. I told Ingrid the story a couple of months ago and she took it upon herself to suggest the mustache to Quinn. He grew one for the heck of it. Nothing to do with me. I promise."

Trevor searched her expression. "So he's on the up-and-up?"

"Very much so. He likes me, but he didn't show up riding a Harley and wearing a mustache because he thought that I'd fall at his feet. He's had the bike for fifteen years and the mustache was Ingrid's idea."

Trevor blew out a breath. "Okay, then."

"Will you please tell your brothers that?"

"Yes, ma'am."

"Thanks, Trevor." She stood on tiptoe and kissed his cheek.

He gave her a quick hug. "Listen, I'd better go, but...do you like *him*?"

"I do."

He smiled. "Then maybe I got it right."

"Yeah, maybe you did."

* * *

After lunch, Kendra made a quick stop at the Crafty Corner so Quinn could pick up a sketchpad. Ryker tagged along because she was his ride back to the ranch, but Badger came because he wanted pointers on what to buy as he launched into scratchboarding.

She would have loved a video of those three broad-shouldered cowboys huddled around the art supplies.

Ryker gazed at Badger in obvious fascination. "All this time and I didn't know this about you, buddy."

"I have hidden depths."

"Apparently."

"But if I hadn't seen Quinn's art, I might not have thought about divin' in to see what's down there. Could be a bunch of old tires and beer cans in those depths."

Quinn laughed. "Or hidden treasure. You won't know until you give it a try."

"I'm gonna do that." Badger gathered up the items Quinn had suggested and started toward the counter. "Reckon Hayley will be surprised."

Kendra fell into step beside him. "I didn't get a chance to ask during lunch. How's her job going?"

"It's goin' well. She's glad the weather's warmin' up, though. Makes the commute to Bozeman easier." He got in the line that had formed at the register. Then he turned back to Quinn, who'd come up behind him. "I don't reckon you've met Hayley."

"I don't think I have. Your girlfriend, I take it?"

"Yes, sir. She's in eldercare, helpin' folks connect with the services they need."

"Nice."

"It is. I look for her to start her own consultin' business soon, so she can expand to underserved areas around the state."

Quinn nodded. "That sounds like a worthy goal."

"She's excited about it. That's where Badger Air comes in. I can fly her wherever she needs to go. And while she's takin' care of business, I'll have this to do." He held up the supplies Quinn had recommended.

Kendra was impressed. "I didn't realize it was part of a whole game plan. You do have hidden depths."

"Yes, ma'am." Badger gave her a quick grin. Then he looked around. "Where'd Cowboy get to?"

"I don't know. I thought he was with us, but...oh, there he is."

Ryker came toward them. He'd taken off his hat, turned it upside down, and loaded the crown with little bags full of something that sparkled.

"Whatcha got there, Cowboy?" Badger called out.

"Beads."

"What for?"

"April keeps saying she wants to make herself some new earrings but she doesn't have time to buy the beads." He walked up to where they stood in line and held out his hat. "Do you think she'll like these?"

Kendra's heart squeezed. "She'll love them." Even if they weren't exactly what she wanted, she'd love Ryker's impulsive decision to buy them for her.

"I don't see how she could help likin' 'em," Badger said. "You've got every color in the rainbow there."

"That was my thinking. Better to have too many choices than not enough." He glanced at Kendra. "What's that smile for?"

"You don't want me to say."

"Why not?"

"It'll embarrass you."

His eyes narrowed. "You think this is sweet, don't you?"

"Yes, and adorable."

He grimaced.

"April will think so, too. It's a very loving gesture and it makes me happy that you're the kind of guy who would fill his hat with sparkly beads for the woman he loves."

"Thanks, Mom. Now I'm *really* embarrassed."

"Told you." She waved a hand toward the register. "Go ahead and get in line. We need to vamoose. I have a lesson in twenty-five minutes."

Outside the Crafty Corner, Quinn gave Badger the names of several videos he could watch to get started. Badger entered the info into his phone, thanked Quinn for all the help and left.

"Who knew?" Ryker asked on the drive back to the ranch. "I never would have guessed ol' Badger wanted to make art."

"I didn't know," Kendra said, "but I'm not totally surprised. He does have hidden depths. Like a lot of people, I guess."

"Well, Mom, I may have hidden depths, but I won't suddenly decide to sculpt or dabble in oils. Just so you know."

"Okay." She flashed him a smile.

"I surprised a lot of people, including myself, when I started," Quinn said. "I was even later to the party than Badger."

"So you just decided one day you were going to get into scratchboarding?"

"Pretty much."

"Had you ever done anything like that before?"

"I took an art class in high school, mostly because the girl I liked was taking it. I'd always doodled and it wasn't a big leap to go from that to seriously trying to draw a realistic picture. I had fun."

"That was it? One class in high school?"

"I took a correspondence course in drawing after I got out of the army, but never did anything with it. Then about ten years ago, I saw my first scratchboard art and knew I had to try it."

"Just like Badger. He told me he'd never seen anything like it until one of your pictures appeared on the wall at the GG. But I thought he just wanted a chance to tell you how much he admired your talent. I had no idea he wanted to do it himself."

"Like I said to him, he's welcome to call me or text if he needs help or advice. I mean it, but he might hesitate to ask. If he talks to you about it, please encourage him to contact me."

"I will. Thanks."

Kendra pulled into the parking area. "Hate to be abrupt, guys, but I gotta run."

"Me, too." Ryker climbed out of the van, his bag of beads in his hand. "I'm doing a maintenance check on the Beechcraft this afternoon. Cody said something about a family dinner Sunday night. Is that a go?"

"It is. Bryce and Nicole aren't performing that night."

"Then I'll make sure April doesn't have anything going on. See you two later." His long strides took him over to his truck.

She reached for the door handle but Quinn was already there, opening her door and offering his hand.

She took it. "Thank you." The pleasure of his firm grip traveled up her arm and spread throughout her body. She stepped down and expected him to move back.

Instead he held his ground. "Interacting with your family has been a kick."

She looked up. Those gray eyes held a special glow again, the one that made her stomach tingle. "I'm glad."

"I'd sure love to kiss you right now."

She allowed her gaze to drift to his mouth. She didn't dare encourage him. He might not blot out the world and lose all track of time when they kissed but she did. "I have a student arriving soon and another is scheduled after that. I have to—"

"I know." He sighed and took a step back. "So I won't. But let the record show that it took a superhuman effort not to."

She nodded.

"See you soon." He turned and started toward the barn.

"Do you have everything you need?"

He turned back. "Not by a long shot." He touched the brim of his hat. "Later, Kendra."

13

Before Quinn started soldering the fuel tank, he returned a couple of calls that had come in while his phone had been silenced. One was from a guy in Bozeman, but it turned out he didn't have the fuel tank model Quinn needed, after all. The lead in Billings was more promising, but in the end Quinn decided the tank they were offering had seen too much hard use to be a safe bet.

This morning Faith had hauled out everything he'd need for the soldering and left it in the stall. He missed having her there as he got started. She likely would have wanted the experience, but she and Cody had an appointment with the minister this afternoon to go over their vows.

Plugging in the soldering iron, he got to work. With critical jobs like this, his focus was so complete that he lost track of time and his surroundings. Only two things affected him that way—working on his bike and scratchboarding.

He'd finished the soldering and was ready to test the job he'd done when he caught a movement from the corner of his eye and he glanced toward the open stall door.

Kendra leaned against it, watching him.

He nudged back his hat and smiled. "Howdy."

"Howdy, yourself."

"How long have you been there?"

"A while. Didn't want to interrupt."

"You could have. It's not like I'm doing heart surgery."

"Bladder surgery?"

He laughed. "Yeah, that fits. I'm about to find out whether the surgery was successful. You can come in, if you want."

"Okay." She walked in and stood on the far side of the bike.

"Are you finished with your lessons?" He picked up the gas can.

"Only one today, after all. The second person cancelled."

"Too bad. I would have liked to watch." After putting some gas in the tank, he crouched down, inspected the tank and swore under this breath.

"That doesn't sound promising."

"It's not. Still leaks, damn it."

"Will you solder it again?"

He shook his head. "There comes a time when you just need to replace a part. I had a hunch that would be the case, but I wanted to try this first."

"How tough will it be to get a fuel tank for a bike this old?"

The comment made him smile. He stood. "Watch your language. She doesn't think she's old."

"She?"

"Yeah. I know it's silly, but—"

"No, it's not. Does she have a name?"

"Cassandra."

"I like it." She folded her arms and surveyed the motorcycle. "Goes with the classy red paint job. She looks like a Cassandra."

He was struck by how naturally Kendra fit into his space, as if she'd been there all along. "I had the strangest feeling just now."

"Oh?" She glanced up.

"Like I've known you for way more than a few months."

She met his gaze. "I've thought that, too. Like I can speak my mind because you'll get it."

"Same here. Or that you might even guess what I'm thinking before I say it."

She nodded.

"Which means you probably know that if I didn't have gas on my hands right now, I'd come over there and kiss you."

Heat flared in her eyes. "We can fix that problem." She walked around the bike. "How about if I kiss you, instead?"

Hot damn. "Okay." His heartbeat kicked into high gear. "I promise not to touch you." He curled his fingers into his palms.

"Thanks." Her mouth tipped up at the corners. "I don't want to smell like gas at tonight's deal."

"Understood."

"But I've been thinking about this all day."

"Me, too."

She cupped his face in her warm hands and her eyes darkened to navy. "I want to know what it feels like without the mustache."

His breath hitched. "Be my guest."

"Technically, you're mine." Dipping her head under the brim of his hat, she touched her soft lips to his.

Oh, yeah, he was hers, all right. She had carte blanche to do whatever she wanted with him. He held on for dear life, his nails biting into his palms as he controlled the fierce desire rolling through him.

She could have made it a chaste kiss, a friendly gesture to test how this worked without the facial hair. But oh, no. She used her tongue to drive him crazy. If her tightening grip and her mounting enthusiasm were any indication, she was going a little crazy, too.

When he began to shake from the effort of keeping his hands to himself, she let him go.

Stepping back, she gulped for air.

So did he, while she stared at him and he stared right back.

She drew in a breath and pressed a hand to her chest. "I should go. I have stuff to do."

"What's the…" He paused to clear his throat. "What's the verdict?"

"On what?"

"Kissing without the 'stache."

"I liked it." She took another deep breath and smiled. "I liked it a lot. Later, Quinn." She skedaddled out of the barn.

Later. He stood immobilized for an embarrassingly long time. *Later.* Maybe she'd meant to tease him. He'd used the same parting shot earlier. Or maybe...

Don't count your chickens, Sawyer. But he couldn't seem to help it. He'd be alone with her after the party tonight. That moment couldn't come soon enough.

* * *

Amazing what one kiss could do. Kendra's energy level spiked as if she'd been swilling espresso all afternoon. She moved through the party preparations like a whirling dervish, outpacing Faith, who'd come up to the house to help her.

Jo arrived a half-hour early to lend a hand and found Kendra and Faith lounging in the living room talking about baby furniture. "You're all ready?"

"We are!" Kendra got up to hug her.

"Someone must've put a quarter in Kendra today." Faith came over for her hug. "I couldn't keep up with her."

"Well, you're supposed to take it easy, anyway." Jo stepped back. "Is the morning sickness bad?"

"Nah. It goes away pretty quick. I think it worries Cody more than it does me."

"And it won't last forever. I'm excited for you." She glanced at Kendra. "And you, too. Here I thought Mandy and Zane would be the first."

"So did I, but Faith and Cody had other plans."

Faith blushed. "Honestly, we didn't expect it to happen so fast. We just—"

"You just wanted a baby." Kendra put her arm around Faith's shoulders. "So did I when Ian and I decided to get married. We—"

"I'm here early, like I promised!" Deidre came in with a flourish as she always did.

"Me, too," Jo said. "Turns out everything's done."

"Well, cover me with feathers and call me a bluebird. Guess we can start drinking." She pulled Faith into a bear hug. "Except for you, sweetheart. Congratulations on the bambino. I should've guessed you'd be the first."

"Well, we—"

"You wanted a baby. And we'll all get to spoil him or her. You're not telling which, right?"

"Right."

"So I suppose we're not allowed to get out the Sacred Ouija Board?" She looked over at Kendra, eyebrows raised.

"No Ouija board. They don't want to know so that's that."

Faith's brow furrowed as she glanced at Kendra. "What's a Ouija board?"

"It's kind of a game." She was surprised that Faith didn't know, but then again it made sense. Faith had been raised in a bunkhouse and hadn't had girlfriends until she'd started working at Wild Creek Ranch.

"Never heard of it."

"Let's show her," Deidre said. "We don't have to do the thing about the baby, but we could ask it something else. I have a million questions about Quinn Sawyer."

That struck fear into Kendra's heart. Just her luck Deidre would be in the middle of asking those embarrassing questions when Quinn came through the door. "I don't know where it is."

"Sure you do," Jo said. "It's in the game closet. I put it away myself the last time we—"

"I've rearranged that closet since then." She gave Jo the evil eye. "I'm pretty sure I tucked it somewhere else."

"Why?"

"Because...it's falling apart, and...we should get a new one."

"A *new* one?" Deidre looked shocked. "This one's part of our history! If we redo the tape, it'll be—" The front door opened as Judy and Christine came in. "Aha! Reinforcements. Guys, Kendra's talking about getting a new Ouija board."

Judy's mouth dropped open. "Why would you do a dumb thing like that?"

"She's just kidding," Christine said. "She wouldn't, really."

Kendra sighed. "No, I wouldn't really. I just—"

"That's a relief." Judy put down her purse. "Is it still in the game closet?"

"Yes, but—"

"Let's get it out. It would be perfect for tonight. We can initiate the newbies into the wonders of the Sacred Ouija Board." She headed down the hallway.

"Wait!" Kendra hurried after her. "Let's not."

"Why?"

"Quinn's coming to the party."

"He is?" Judy opened the closet door and turned back to her. "Excellent. But what's that got to do with the Ouija board?"

"He's a guy."

"I noticed that. I'm quick that way." She opened the closet door and pulled out the Ouija board, which sat right on top of the stack. Carrying the tattered box, she started toward the living room. "I can't imagine getting a new one, but I'll admit a few more pieces of tape would improve the situation."

"Let me grab some out of my office."

"I'll go with you." Judy followed her inside. "How's it going with Quinn?"

"We've kissed. Twice." She opened her desk drawer and took out the tape dispenser.

"That's all?"

She closed the drawer and glanced at Judy. "I think that's a lot, considering I haven't kissed anyone since Ian."

"True. Was it fun?"

"Yes."

Happiness bloomed on Judy's round face. "That's wonderful. You deserve this."

"Jo said that."

"Jo's right and you need to mellow out and enjoy yourself."

She took a deep breath. "Good advice. Let's tape up this battered relic and introduce it to the next generation of true believers."

Twenty minutes later the box was repaired and Faith's attendants –Mandy, April,

Nicole and Olivia—had all arrived. Drinks were being served when a recently shaved and showered Quinn walked through her front door.

He moved smoothly into the flow of activity, his smile relaxed and easy as he greeted everyone. She stood with a wine glass in each hand, mesmerized.

At last his gaze found hers. And held. In that second she was many things—dizzy, shaky, hot and breathless. But mellow? Not a chance.

14

Quinn was having a blast. He'd always liked the company of women and this batch was hilarious. The wine that flowed freely during the evening didn't hurt, but he'd likely get a kick out of these ladies whether they were tipsy or sober.

He enjoyed the stimulation of being in the same room with Kendra even if he couldn't act on the impulses that bombarded him whenever he glanced her way. She didn't look at him much, but whenever she did, the air crackled between them. No doubt her friends took notice of those hot exchanges.

Judging from the cheerful way everyone treated him, they didn't mind that he was clearly enamored of their beloved friend. And she was beloved, by those who'd known her for more than forty years and those she'd met recently.

After dinner, the table was cleared so they could make the favors. Faith and Kendra brought out bird seed and drawstring bags with little tags attached.

"We need a volunteer with good handwriting to put *Faith and Cody* plus the date on the tags," Kendra announced.

Christine, the tall blonde who'd known Kendra since kindergarten, spoke up first. "Since we have an artist among us, I nominate Quinn for the job."

"Brilliant idea." Deidre, the apparent ringleader of the Whine and Cheese Club, focused on Quinn. "That's if you're willing."

"Happy to. I bought some colored pencils today at the Crafty Corner. Let me go fetch them." He pushed back his chair and stood.

"Perfect." Christine sent him a smile of approval. "We'll start filling the bags while you're gone."

"Sounds like a plan." He headed for the front door and grabbed his hat from the coat tree.

"Why don't you go with him, Kendra?" Jo said casually.

Thank you, Jo. Great suggestion. He paused, his handle on the knob, and glanced back at Kendra.

She looked adorably flustered. "I doubt you need help carrying a box of pencils."

"I don't, but I wouldn't mind the company."

"Then, sure, I'll go." Color high, Kendra left her chair and started toward him.

"But don't forget to come back." Faith smiled at Quinn. "I want fancy writing on the tags."

"We'll be back." He opened the door and followed Kendra outside.

She turned to him after he'd closed the door. "They can't resist," she said in a low voice.

"Do you mind?"

She gave him a cute little smile. "Truthfully? No."

"Temperature's dropping. Think I'll grab my jacket along with the pencils."

"Maybe I should go back and get my—"

"No need." He put his arm around her shoulders and started toward the steps. "I'll keep you warm until we get to the cabin. You can wear mine on the return trip."

"Um, okay." She slipped her arm around his waist and tucked in closer.

Her warmth and the sweet aroma of her body nearly undid him. Somehow he managed to make pleasant conversation. "Thank you for letting me come to this party. It's a great group."

"They're pretty happy with you, too."

"I'm glad they are. I have a suspicion that if they weren't, my chances with you would suffer."

"I've known my girlfriends a long time. Mandy and April, too. The others are more recent, but Faith is like a daughter to me and Olivia's a trusted friend. Nicole inspired Bryce to take up his guitar again, which I'm incredibly grateful for. I love them all so much."

"They love you right back. But it's no wonder. You're like a magnet drawing out the good in people." In his case, she also inspired a hotter, more potent energy, one that swirled around them now.

"Thank you." She sounded breathless, but then again, they were climbing the slope to the cabin. "By the way, in case you wondered about

Trevor showing up at the GG and wanting to discuss—"

"My mustache? Yeah, what was that all about?"

"Months ago he made this prediction that a mustache-wearing guy would ride into town on a motorcycle and sweep me off my feet."

"No kidding?" He laughed. "That's wild."

"Wait, there's more. I mentioned this to Ingrid and Abigail in February after I met you, which is why Ingrid called Roxanne while you guys were eating lunch at the GG."

"And asked if I had a motorcycle."

"Right. It's also why she suggested that you grow a mustache."

"Oh, man." He shook his head. "I had no idea all that was going on."

"But my boys didn't know you were clueless. They thought maybe you'd added the mustache on purpose, to fit the profile."

"Do they still think that?"

"I doubt it. That's why I took Trevor aside today, to set him straight and ask him to pass the word."

"Thanks." He glanced down at her. "You said he came up with this scenario?"

"Uh-huh."

"What did you think of it?"

"I was intrigued."

"And now?"

She smiled. "Even more intrigued."

"Guess I owe your son a debt of gratitude for paving the way for me."

"Don't tell him that."

He chuckled. "Wasn't going to." Clouds and the shadow of tall pines darkened the path and he walked carefully until they stepped into the glow from the porch light. He'd left a lamp on inside the cabin, too.

The place always looked cozy, but never more so than now, with Kendra by his side. "If I hadn't promised to go back and decorate those tags and you weren't the hostess of the party, I'd invite you inside."

"But you did and I am."

"Then you'd better wait on the porch." He kept her tucked against his hip as they climbed the steps. "I'll be right out."

"Is the cabin working well for you?"

"I love it." He released her and ducked inside before his noble intentions vanished in a wave of hot desire. He didn't dare spend time with her in such close quarters, especially when the space included a bed.

Grabbing the box of pencils and his denim jacket, he stepped outside.

She stood with her arms folded and her back to him, gazing down through the trees to the ranch house, its windows alight and the faint sound of animated voices and laughter drifting on the breeze.

He paused, struck by the image of Kendra as a precious jewel in a perfect setting—Wild Creek Ranch. She was the heart and soul of this place. Regardless of what happened between them, he'd be wise to keep that in mind.

He closed the door with a muted click and she faced him with a soft smile of welcome. The porch light caught the intense blue of her eyes and the sprinkling of silver in her hair. Damn, she was beautiful.

Shoving the box of pencils in his hip pocket, he shook out his jacket and held it for her.

"Thanks." She pivoted and slipped her arms into sleeves that hung down past her hands. "You know, I halfway expected you to ride into town wearing a black leather one."

"Was that part of Trevor's prediction?" He lifted the jacket onto her shoulders. He could fit two of her in it.

"We didn't get into clothing choices."

"I have a leather one but I'm partial to denim."

"Me, too." She turned back to him and pushed up the sleeves. "Thanks for the loan."

"Anytime." He nudged back his hat. "Just so you know, I don't plan to leave this porch without kissing you."

She closed the gap between them and rested her palms against his chest. "I was hoping you had that in mind."

"Always." Easing his hands inside the unbuttoned jacket, he drew her closer.

She gazed up at him. "Your heart's beating really fast."

"Tell me something I don't know."

"All right." She took a quick breath. "Mine's beating even faster." She wound her arms around his neck.

"Glad to hear it." Lowering his head, he captured her mouth. Mm. He settled in, exploring and savoring the moist warmth and sweet taste of her with a smooth slide of his tongue.

So good. And getting better. He shifted the angle and went back for more. She was deliciously eager. Blood pounded in his ears, blocking out everything but her whimper of pleasure when he nibbled on her lips and her gasp of excitement when he thrust his tongue deep.

The rapid pace of her breathing matched his and her arms tightened, crushing her breasts against the wall of his chest. He cupped her bottom and pulled her firmly against his needy package. It was a wonder he didn't set her jeans on fire.

Lifting his mouth a fraction from hers, he gulped in a breath. "We'd better stop."

"I know." She swallowed. "We can't...this isn't..." She moaned and pulled his head down.

He surrendered to her hot mouth as flames licked at the edges of his control. Pressing his fingers into her taut behind, he rocked his hips forward. Desire battled duty. A bed was only steps away.

Duty won. He lifted his head. Struggling for air, he took a step back while holding her steady so she wouldn't fall.

Slowly her eyes opened, and the heat in those blue depths made him tremble. She sucked in a ragged breath, moved back and leaned against the porch railing. "I've come to a decision."

He waited, heart pounding.

"I want to make love tomorrow night."

"*Tomorrow* night?"

"Yes, please."

"Why not—" He stopped himself from saying it. Maybe she needed twenty-four hours to adjust to the idea. If so, he'd honor that.

"Were you about to ask me why not tonight?"

"Yes, ma'am, but if you need time, that's perfectly fine. No worries. Tomorrow night it is. I'll look forward to it." Gross understatement. He'd be counting the seconds.

"I'm not the one who needs time, but I thought you would."

"Me?"

"You know." She looked at him as if he was one donut shy of a dozen. "To go shopping."

"Shopping?" He stared at her in confusion. "Would you like me to bring you a gift?"

"Good grief, no. I'm talking about condoms."

"*Oh.*" Blew that call.

"If you have some on hand I'll be very surprised. You don't seem like the type to be constantly prepared."

"I'm not. It's been years since my last...anyway, Anne and I decided four kids was enough so I had the procedure."

"I see." Her cheeks turned pink. "Well, that's good to know."

"I've got a clean bill of health, but I can pick some up tomorrow."

"Not necessary."

"So, um...how does that affect the timetable?"

Her breath caught. "I guess we don't have to wait, then."

"No." He hesitated. "But we don't have to barrel forward, either." Much as he'd like to. "This is a big step for you."

She nodded. "When we're kissing, I'm ready to rock and roll, but—"

"We've just had *the talk*, which can be a major buzz kill."

"You really want to, though. I can tell."

"Yes, I really want to. But that's not your problem." He held out his hand. "Let's go back, finish making the favors, and take things as they come."

She laced her fingers through his as they started down the porch steps. "You're a good guy, Quinn."

He gave her hand a squeeze. "Thanks, but I'm no choir boy. If kisses make you want to rock and roll, I'll be sure and steal a few before the night's over."

15

Kendra prepared herself for some teasing when she and Quinn came back much later than a quick trip for pencils would require. Surely everyone knew they'd been making out.

She hadn't bothered to put on lipstick before everyone arrived tonight, so the physical evidence wouldn't be too obvious. But they'd been gone quite a while and chances were good she was flushed. Nobody said a word.

This romance clearly had their blessing. Too bad her sons didn't feel the same way. She hadn't mentioned it to Quinn, but that was another reason why, given a chance to cool down, she became hesitant about making the decision to have sex with him.

Although she was a grown woman with the right to make her own choices, she was hesitant about letting her boys know that Quinn had shared her bed. Or that she'd shared his if they chose the cabin, instead. Her boys didn't seem comfortable with it. Understandable. She wasn't completely comfortable with it, either.

After hanging Quinn's jacket on the coat tree next to where he'd put his hat, she reclaimed her place at the table. Then she threw herself into party mode, filling little bags with seed and participating in the conversational threads. Quinn was seated across from her and he immediately started on the tags.

He'd finished several before Faith picked up a finished bag and looked at the tag. "Aw, Quinn, that's adorable!" She passed the bag to Mandy, who was sitting next to her. "Look at what he drew on the back of the tags."

Mandy smiled. "Lovebirds. That's just precious."

"Oh, look!" Faith showed her another one. "They're not even all the same!"

"Wow." April spread several out on the table. "Quinn, this is spectacular. No two are alike. These will become keepsakes."

Quinn smiled. "There's no way I could make them all the same, anyway, so might as well make them different on purpose."

"I get that. When I make a pair of earrings, I try so hard to make them match exactly, but they never do." She glanced at Kendra. "Which reminds me, are you the one who suggested to Ryker that he could buy me some beads?"

"That was all his idea."

"That's even more touching, then."

Mandy gaped at her. "Ryker bought you beads from Crafty Corner?"

"Yes, and they're wonderful. A rainbow of colors. I can't wait to start working with them." She looked over at Quinn. "Maybe it was partly your doing, then."

Quinn shook his head. "I did absolutely nothing, except maybe getting him into the store."

"That alone is a miracle. I doubt he's set foot in there until today. And he said Badger was taking up scratchboarding thanks to you. You're a good influence, Quinn."

"Thank you, ma'am, but I—"

"You absolutely are," Deidre said. "You can't get more manly than riding and maintaining a badass Harley. But you're also an accomplished artist. It's good for the young guys around here to see that they don't have to be one-dimensional. Creativity is sexy."

Kendra expected at least an eyebrow waggling glance in her direction after that remark if not a pointed *right, Kendra?* Didn't happen.

Clearly Deidre was exercising restraint and that was unusual. Kendra was dying to ask what that was all about and she got her chance when the favors were almost done and she left the table to organize coffee and dessert. Deidre came in to help but everyone else stayed put.

Evidently that was intentional, because as they took out plates for the large sheet cake Jo had made, Deidre lowered her voice. "I can tell you want to know what's up."

"Sure do." She measured coffee beans and put them in the grinder.

"When Jo sent you off with Quinn, we all had a golden opportunity to discuss this situation."

Kendra rolled her eyes. "Why am I not surprised you did that?"

"Just be quiet and listen. We all concluded that this was a fabulous opportunity for you, regardless of whether it lasted a few days or ten years. We want you to go for it, even if your boys are acting a wee bit territorial."

"You can't blame them. They've never seen me involved with a man other than their father, and Ryker and Zane are the only ones who even remember that."

"Nobody's blaming them. It's perfectly natural that they're feeling protective of you and uneasy about Quinn. We're just prepared to neutralize their response."

"*What*?"

"You have allies, sweetie, women who will run interference for you. Mandy and Jo will double-team Zane. April's got Ryker covered, Nicole's going to monitor Bryce, and Faith's in charge of Cody. Olivia doesn't anticipate much resistance from Trevor since he's the one who was urging you to date."

"But talking about it is a whole different thing from actually seeing it happen. I don't think he's as enamored of the idea as he thought he'd be."

"Doesn't matter. We understand how difficult it might be for you to face them and assert your right to have a healthy sexual adventure, but we—"

"You're going to say it like that?" She was horrified.

"Of course not. Everyone will be subtle. The goal is to gently bring them around so you don't have to be embarrassed about getting it on with that gorgeous man in there."

Kendra dumped the ground coffee in the basket. "He is gorgeous."

"No kidding." Deidre cut and dished the cake with the efficiency of a seasoned hostess. "Do you two have a plan?"

"Uh..."

"No plan?"

"We've decided to see how it goes."

Deidre turned to stare at her. "Seriously?"

"Shh!"

Deidre lowered the volume. "Kendra, the man has obligations. He doesn't have the luxury of hanging around Wild Creek Ranch for days to *see how it goes.*"

"I understand that and...and it's possible that it could be...tonight." Her heart bounced in her chest like a Mexican jumping bean.

"That's more like it. Then Mandy and Faith can caution Zane and Cody not to react if they show up to feed and notice Quinn coming out of the house first thing in the morning."

"He *won't.* I'll send him back to his cabin *long* before then. That's if we even have sex tonight. One minute I want to and the next minute I've changed my mind."

Deidre put down the knife and came over to give her a hug. "I know. Keep the lights low for the first time, until you get used to it again. I promise it won't take long for you to embrace your inner vixen. You're a lovely, sensual woman and I guarantee he thinks so, too."

"Thank you." Deidre's hug soothed her. "Jo told me to just go for it, but that's easy for her to say. She'd be as much of a chicken as I am if some man became interested in her."

Deidre chuckled. "You've got that right."

"You're not chicken, though. And how we teased you about Jim. I feel bad about that, now."

"Ah, I didn't mind. It was all in fun. But let me tell you, I was very nervous the first time with him."

"How did you handle that?"

"I looked into his eyes. That man wanted me more than he wanted to draw his next breath. Then it wasn't about me. It was about making him happy and boy, did I ever." Deidre chuckled. "You'll make Quinn extremely happy. Focus on that."

Kendra gazed at her. "You're a very wise lady."

"Sometimes." She grinned. "Other times I'm full of crap. Let's serve this cake."

They returned to the dining room. All the bags had been filled and moved to the end of the table where Quinn was still decorating the tags. At the other end sat the Ouija board.

Okay, she wouldn't panic. Deidre had just assured her that the women in the room wished for a good outcome for her and Quinn. Embarrassing either of them made no sense.

"If you can believe it, April's the only one who's ever fooled around with a Ouija board," Judy said. "Nicole and Olivia were both taught it was woo-woo nonsense, and Mandy—"

"I didn't think it was nonsense," Mandy said. "I just didn't want to know what it might tell me back then. But life's good, now, so I'm game."

"I just looked it up on my phone," Olivia said. "Not everybody thinks it's nonsense. Some scientists consider it a tool for accessing the subconscious. That's kind of cool."

Kendra peeked over at Quinn to see how he was taking this. If his relaxed body language was any indication, he wasn't the least bit uncomfortable.

As if sensing her interest, he glanced her way. His gray eyes twinkled and his mouth curved in an intimate smile clearly meant only for her.

Her body clenched with a fierce longing that left her breathless. His hands stilled as the twinkle in his eyes gradually changed to fire. And she wanted everyone gone. Immediately if not sooner.

"We're going to start with Mandy and Faith," Judy said.

Making a supreme effort, Kendra broke eye contact with Quinn and concentrated on the rest of her guests, who had not magically disappeared, after all.

"The most recently married and the about to be married seems like a good pairing," Judy continued. "Ladies, place your fingertips on the planchette."

Faith looked up. "The what?"

"That little footed triangular thing with the magnifier in the middle," Mandy said.

"We just called it a pointer." April had left her chair to stand behind Mandy and lean over her shoulder. "But I like calling it a planchette. Makes me feel French."

As in French kissing. Kendra didn't look at Quinn in case he'd also been reminded of the activity that had recently taken place on the cabin's front porch. They couldn't keep exchanging hot glances without eventually getting caught.

"Light touch, ladies," Judy said. "Get your questions ready. The Sacred Ouija Board is at your service."

Soon Faith and Mandy were both giggling as the planchette zipped around the board, seemingly under its own power. They got answers to everything from *Is the wedding night all that important? (YES)* to *When will Mandy get pregnant? (SOON)*.

Olivia and Nicole took the next turn, peppering the board with their questions. Everyone cheered when Nicole got a *YES* when she asked whether she and Bryce would have a hit recording in the next year. Olivia smiled after she asked how many children she'd have with Trevor and the answer was *4*.

Nicole glanced across the table at her. "I could swear I heard Trevor say he wanted two."

"We're still in negotiations. Looks like I might convince him, after all." She moved out of her chair. "Who's next?"

Judy looked over at Quinn. "You seem to be finished with the tags."

"Yes, ma'am. Just did."

"I'll bet you've never messed around with a Ouija board."

"Sure haven't."

"That makes you the last Ouija board virgin in the group."

"Can't have that." He unfolded himself from his chair and stood. "Kendra, want to show me how it's done?"

<u>16</u>

Quinn got a charge out of Kendra's shell-shocked expression. Evidently she'd expected him to gracefully refuse. But ever since Judy had set up the board, he'd had a hunch she'd challenge him to try it. As one of Kendra's oldest friends, she'd want to test his mettle.

Picking up on Judy's likely intention had given him valuable time to decide whether he'd agree or not. He'd been ready to say yes, and at the last minute had chosen to take the initiative.

Judy might have paired him with Kendra, but that wasn't guaranteed. Judy's wry sense of humor might have caused her to suggest Deidre or maybe even herself. If he was going to do this, might as well be with Kendra. Then they'd be in it together.

She had to move from one chair to another, and he helped her with that before rounding the table and taking a seat on the other side. Her color was high, but she didn't look scared. Now that she was over the initial shock, he read amusement in those bright eyes.

Judy instructed them to rest their fingers on the planchette.

His were larger than Kendra's and he encroached on her space. Couldn't help it. Didn't care. If all he could touch were her fingertips, he'd take what he could get.

"Get your questions ready," Judy said. "The Sacred Ouija Board is at your service."

Kendra got the jump on him. "I have one. Sacred Ouija Board, what's Quinn's favorite color?"

The planchette began to scoot across the board, although Quinn swore he wasn't doing it. "Kendra, are you making it move?"

"Nope. I have no idea what your favorite color is. I could guess red because of your motorcycle, but—" The planchette paused over the *B*. "Not red, then."

The darned thing kept going and paused over the *L* before finishing up with a stop at the *U* and the *E*.

Kendra looked at him. "Is that right?"

"Yes. But I don't know how it did that."

"I read some more on it just now," Olivia said. "It's called the ideomotor effect. You don't think you're making it move, but your muscles are reacting without you telling them to. Or something like that."

Quinn frowned. "I swear I didn't make it spell out *blue*. All right. I'll ask it something I don't know. What's Kendra's—"

"Hang on," Judy said. "You have to address it correctly. Say *Sacred Ouija Board* first and then ask your question."

He glanced at Kendra and smiled. "Do I get points for this?"

"I don't know about Kendra," Deidre said, "but you're getting a boatload of points from me."

Kendra's eyes sparkled with mischief. "Depends on your question."

"Then I better make it a good one." He cleared his throat. "Sacred Ouija Board, what's Kendra's favorite gemstone?"

"Be still my heart," Christine said. "The man's contemplating a jewelry purchase."

The planchette remained stationary.

"Kendra," Judy used the sing-song tone of a parent scolding a child. "What are you doing?"

"Trying to make it spell *rhinestone* but it won't."

He grinned. "I'm shocked that you'd try to mislead the Sacred Ouija Board."

"Not mislead. Outwit. I figure if I concentrate hard enough on my answer, it'll just do it."

"But it never does," Deidre said. "Because it's coming from your conscious mind not your subconscious. Repeat your question, Quinn. Kendra, let the planchette work."

She blew out a breath. "Okay."

Quinn asked again and this time the planchette quickly spelled *OPAL*. Not a common choice. "Why opal?"

"It's my birthstone, for one thing."

"And that's for..."

"October. I love fire opals, especially. At first they might look sort of plain, just milky white, but when they catch the light, they flash with brilliant color."

"I never noticed that." This Ouija board deal had its uses. He could find out all sorts of things about her. "Sacred Ouija Board, what's Kendra's—"

"Wait," Judy said. "It's Kendra's turn."

"Oh. Sorry. Got carried away."

Kendra stared into space for a moment. "All right, I have one. Sacred Ouija Board, what's Quinn's favorite place?"

Quinn deliberately kept his touch light as a feather. He had no idea how he'd answer that. He loved the Lazy S, so likely that would be what came up. But he'd found some awesome spots in his travels on the Harley, too, like that cabin hideaway in the Cascades, his favorite beach near Anacortes, the fire pit here on Wild Creek Ranch...

The planchette spelled *W-I-T-H-K-M* and stopped.

Kendra frowned. "That's not a place, unless it's an acronym, or there's some Native American site near your ranch where you—"

"It's a place," Quinn said quietly.

Deidre came over and rested her hand on Kendra's shoulder. "It sure is, sweetie. Put a break between the *H* and the *K*."

"With KM?" Her eyes widened and she clapped a hand over her mouth as a collective sigh went up from the group.

He didn't know what to do. He hadn't intended to reveal so much, and especially not in front of so many people. Her question had been innocent enough. She might have been curious to find out if he loved his ranch as much as she loved hers. Evidently not.

"Hey, it's getting late," Judy said. "I don't know about you guys, but tomorrow's a busy Friday for me. I need to call it a night."

"Same here." Deidre started gathering up dessert plates and coffee mugs. "I'm showing a house first thing in the morning."

"And I need to be at the bank early," Jo said. "Staff meeting."

Quinn snapped out of his daze and got up so he could gather dishes and mugs.

Kendra whipped into action, too. "I'll get a box for the favors. The tags look fabulous, Quinn." She didn't look at him as she said it.

"Thanks. It was fun."

Judy packed up the Ouija board in a box that was more tape than cardboard.

Quinn paused, a stack of plates in one hand and his fingers looped through the handles of three mugs. "How old is that board, anyway?"

"I gave it to Kendra for her fourteenth birthday, so that makes it older than any of the sweet young things who are here tonight."

"I'm glad you got it out." Mandy wrapped an arm around Judy's shoulders and gave her a sideways hug. "I can't wait to tell Zane that the Sacred Ouija Board said we're going to be pregnant soon."

Jo laughed. "Can I be there and take a video? Please?"

"Sure!"

Faith glanced up from the box where she and Kendra were carefully stacking the seed bags. "I can't wait to tell Cody that our wedding night needs to be spectacular."

"If I know that boy," Kendra said, "and I do, he's planning to pull out all the stops."

Quinn wasn't sure what *pulling out all the stops* meant to Kendra and he wished he had that info. The women were leaving him alone with her, quite likely because they believed something significant would happen tonight. He wanted them to be right.

But he couldn't get a fix on her current emotional state. The message from the Ouija board might have freaked her out. It had surprised him, too, but he hadn't been shocked.

If Olivia's Internet research was valid and working with the board had pulled something out of his subconscious, he'd better listen up. His subconscious was telling him that Kendra was a significant part of his life, whether he was ready to admit that or not.

In record time, the dishwasher was running and the kitchen was spotless. Kendra had put away the box of favors and the surface of the massive dining table that had been the center of all the activity was now a gleaming slab of hardwood with not even a cake crumb to mar its perfection.

The guests didn't waste much time making tracks for home, either. They said goodbye to him as if assuming he wouldn't be leaving. He didn't want to, but he wasn't in charge of that decision.

The last person out the door was Jo, who hugged Kendra and said something that Quinn couldn't hear.

But Kendra's reply was clear as a bell. "Don't worry. I won't." She closed the door and turned to him.

"Won't what?"

"She told me not to be an idiot." She shoved her hands in the front pockets of her jeans.

"Meaning?"

Her breathing quickened. "Don't let something wonderful pass me by."

His spirits lifted. "That sounds like good advice." Maybe, just maybe—

"Oh, it is, but..." She paused to take a shaky breath. "We need to get something straight."

"Okay." He'd agree to any terms she laid out.

"I'm not looking for a husband."

He nodded. "Understood."

"I'm not looking for a live-in boyfriend, either."

"Since I already have a place to live, that would be difficult for me to manage, anyway."

"I know that, but when the Ouija board—"

"Even if that thing's accurate and my favorite place is with you, that doesn't mean I require your presence to be happy. Apples are my favorite food, but I don't eat them with every—"

"*Apples*? You're kidding."

He shrugged. "What can I say? I grew up in Washington." He stepped closer. "If you're worried that I'll become a pest, don't be. Not my style."

"I know that, too." She hesitated, her gaze uncertain. "But maybe it's premature to..."

"What?"

She spoke quickly, clearly nervous. "You have a life in Spokane and I have mine here. Just because we enjoy each other's company doesn't mean we have to see each other all the time or change our situation." She swallowed. "Right?"

"Right. We can just visit." It made sense. It wasn't the warm and fuzzy solution where two people settled under the same roof, but that move was easier for twenty-somethings who hadn't built a life yet.

Her chest heaved. "Exactly. But we'd have to test it and see, I guess."

"Got any ideas about how we could begin testing it?" He moved within a foot of her, near enough that he was in range of her warmth and her womanly scent. His nostrils flared.

"I suppose that's obvious."

"Is it?" He'd managed to keep his desire in check until now, but he couldn't guarantee how much longer that would work for him. If she wanted to hold off until tomorrow night, he'd have to head for the cabin immediately and take a cold shower.

"I mean, we don't even know if we're…sexually compatible."

"True." His groin tightened. "And I think there's only one way to—"

"Then let's do this." She held out her hand. It was shaking.

He captured that quivering hand and brought it to his lips. "I'd be happier about that invitation if you didn't look as if you were marching off to have a tooth pulled."

Her gaze lifted to his and a pulse beat rapidly in the hollow of her throat. "It's been a long time."

"I know." And getting longer by the second. He nibbled on her fingers. "But we'll take it easy. You can direct the—"

"Dear God, that would be worse."

"It would?"

"Earlier tonight, when everyone was here and you gave me that hot look, I was ready to jump your bones, but now they're all gone and the moment of truth has arrived...I'm...just kiss me, okay?"

"That I can do." He drew her gently into his arms and cradled her cheek in one hand while he held her tight with the other. She gripped the front of his shirt with both hands. She was trembling as he lowered his head and settled his mouth over hers.

Resisting the urge to hurry, he took his time. He traced the seam of her lips with the tip of his tongue and coaxed his way in as she slowly relaxed. Gradually her body molded with his and her mouth offered the warm welcome she'd given him earlier tonight.

Loosening her grip on his shirt, she slid her hands around his neck and cupped the back of his head. Taking that as a good sign, he deepened the kiss.

And she caught fire. With a low moan, she pressed her fingertips into his scalp. When she began sucking on his tongue, he knew it was time to move the party.

Scooping her up in his arms, he started toward the hallway.

She broke away from his kiss. "Do you know where you're going?"

"Yes, ma'am. I'm taking you to bed."

_17_

This was happening. Kendra held on tight as Quinn's long strides took him to the end of the hall. She wanted this. She really did. Her panties were damp and her skin tingled, but she wished they could be magically naked and under the covers.

Quinn didn't ask for directions, but then the location of the master bedroom wouldn't be a mystery in a layout like this one. And hers was the only room with a light on.

She'd turned on a bedside table lamp after she'd freshened up for the party. It provided the subdued illumination Deidre had recommended. But what came next?

They were both still wearing boots, and all their clothes. Married sex had been so simple—get undressed and climb into...

Quinn set her gently on the edge of the bed. "Let me get your boots." He dropped to his knees in front of her.

She gulped. "Okay." Her heart was beating so fast that she could barely breathe. What had Deidre told her to do? _Look into his eyes._

But he'd lowered his head while he picked up her foot and tugged off her boot and her sock. He set both aside and repeated the action on her other foot.

"What about your boots?"

He glanced up. "Thought I'd take them off, too."

"How about now?"

"I could." Amusement flashed in his eyes. "Boots are the tricky part, aren't they?"

She nodded.

"Then let's get the tricky part over with." He sat beside her and took off both his boots and his socks, leaving his feet bare.

She stared in fascination. His toes were nicely shaped, the nails neatly trimmed. "There's something so...intimate about bare feet."

Reaching for her hand, he laced his fingers through hers. "I like your feet."

She sucked in air. "I like yours, too."

"Do you want to sit here for a minute? Catch your breath?"

"Yes. No. I don't know. This used to be like falling off a log, but after all this time I don't—"

"I have an idea."

That made her smile. "I'll bet you do."

"What if we start with you undressing me?"

Ah. After being plastered against his lovely broad chest and firm abs, she could guess how great he'd look without a shirt. His muscled thighs had stretched the denim of his jeans when he'd crouched beside his motorcycle today. She wouldn't mind seeing him without his jeans.

As for what was behind the fly of his jeans…her core ached with longing. After years of deprivation, she wanted a glimpse of that, too. She looked over at him. "I like your idea."

"Thought you might." He let go of her hand. Standing, he faced her, stepped back and spread his arms. "I'm all yours."

She shivered with anticipation as she rose slowly to her feet. All that lovely territory, hers to explore. She tapped her finger against her lip. "Where to start, where to start."

"I suggest starting at the top and working your way down. If you go straight for the middle…chaos."

"There does seem to be a storm brewing in that area."

"Don't make fun."

"I'm not." She held his gaze and heat sluiced through her. That was the look Deidre had been talking about—barely contained, primal need. Need she could satisfy. Wanted to satisfy. "I like storms."

"Yeah." His voice was husky. "Me, too."

"Thunder. Lightning." She closed the distance between them and reached for his wrist to unsnap his cuffs. "Exciting stuff."

"Yes, ma'am." He held out his other wrist.

"Thanks." She breathed in the scent of soap, a piney aftershave and the musk of desire. She'd been too stressed to take notice before, but now that the focus was on his manly self she could fully appreciate…everything.

"If there's anything I can do to help, just let me know."

"I've got this." She tugged his shirttails from the waistband of his jeans. The blue plaid was faded and wear-softened. "Favorite shirt?"

"Uh-huh." His chest heaved.

She glanced up at him. "Are you okay?"

"Keeping my hands to myself is tougher than I thought it would be." He gave her a wry smile.

"Want to do this yourself?"

"No. But don't stop, please."

"Okay." She started working on the snaps. Oh, baby, no t-shirt. Every popped snap revealed more of his extremely touchable pecs that quivered with each ragged breath. But he'd asked her not to stop, so there was no time to admire, let alone touch, that tempting expanse with its sprinkling of chest hair touched with gray.

She worked faster, finished undoing the snaps and pushed the shirt off his broad shoulders. She had to stand on tiptoe to do it and her mouth accidentally grazed his skin.

He groaned.

"Sorry." But she wasn't. Her lips tingled from the contact. She wanted to do it again, to rain kisses all over that sculpted, manly chest.

"Just keep going."

She snapped out of her daze. "I should fold up your—"

"Toss it on the floor."

"Right." Passion simmered in her core. She tackled his belt next and couldn't seem to manage it, maybe because she was starting to shake. At last she backed away from him. "You'll have to do it."

He gave a quick nod and unbuckled it.

"The rest, too." She no longer had the time or patience.   A deep, persistent craving had overridden every hesitation.

"Are you sure?"

"Yes." Unbuttoning her blouse wasn't easy, either, but she did it.

"Are you getting undressed?"

"Yep." She stripped off her jeans. She wanted nothing to get in the way. "I want you so much I'm ready to spontaneously combust." She whipped off her bra and her damp panties.

He stood very still and fire burned in his gaze. "You're amazing."

"Please get out of your clothes and come to bed."

"You've got it."

She tossed back the covers and climbed in, dazzled by the promise of making love to the man striding toward her.

Magnificent. Strong, bold, and fully aroused. She opened her arms, and he came straight into them, his sigh rich with pleasure.

Braced above her, he leaned down and gave her a lingering, open-mouthed kiss. The slight trembling of his body betrayed the effort he was making to hold himself in check. He drew back. "I should probably take it slow this first time." His voice was tight with strain.

"Don't you dare, Quinn Sawyer."

"Oh?"

"I don't want slow and careful." She stroked both hands down his muscled back and cupped his tight butt. "And neither do you."

"No, but I—"

"I've waited a long time for you. Give me wild and crazy, hot and heavy."

"Thank God." He probed once and hesitated only long enough for his gaze to lock onto hers. Then he sank deep with a groan of happiness.

She gasped. "Oh, my."

"Okay?"

"More than okay. More than I ever...oh, Quinn." Words failed her.

"I knew it." He eased back and rocked forward again. "I knew we'd be like this."

"I...didn't." The wonder of it overwhelmed her. "I didn't know."

"And now you do." He began to stroke. "I believe you requested wild and crazy."

Her breath hitched. "I did."

"Hot and heavy."

"That, too."

"Hold on. I'm about to grant that request." He settled in, his chest brushing the tips of her breasts as he picked up the pace.

She caught his rhythm, rising to meet each thrust, intensifying the friction deep in her body and across her newly sensitized nipples. His breath roughened as he drove in even faster, rocking the bed until the wood squeaked and the headboard rattled.

The clench of an impending orgasm brought a cry from her lips. He bore down and she abandoned herself to a blizzard of sensation, spinning in a vortex he created, calling his name over and over.

As the intensity of her climax ebbed, he slowed, only to gulp for air and pick up speed. "Again, Kendra. Again!" His hoarse command blended with the frenzied creaks and thumps from the rocking bedframe and the quivering mattress.

She reveled in the erotic sounds of harsh breathing, moist bodies repeatedly connecting, and the bedframe keeping time with the frantic beat. Coaxed back to the summit, she joyfully surrendered to a second powerful orgasm as he urged her on. The waves rolled over her and she arched into his final deliberate thrust with a jubilant cry.

He came, then, too, his bellow of satisfaction filling the bedroom with masculine energy. Shuddering in her arms, he gasped out her name. And closed his eyes.

Stroking his sweaty back, she studied his face at close range. She admired his deep-set eyes and high cheekbones, his strong jaw and perfectly proportioned mouth. He was handsome, no question about that.

But he had more going for him than pleasing looks. Character was etched into that face. Lines fanning out from the corners of his eyes were the result of hours spent monitoring the ranch and his horses. Grooves in his cheeks testified that he loved to laugh and smile. Twin frown lines sat prominently between his eyebrows. His life had not been worry-free.

She understood all those lines because she shared them. No wonder they'd been drawn to each other. They'd lived a similar life.

His eyes fluttered open. "Hey." His voice was low and intimate. Damn sexy.

"Hey, yourself." She smiled. "Thanks for honoring my request."

"It was easy. Like falling off a log."

"Easy, really?" She massaged his back. "You worked up quite a sweat."

"Ask me if I mind. I was in a lather from the moment we came into this room, but I kept telling myself to be careful. Not to rush. To give you time to adjust to being with a man again."

"I do believe I've adjusted."

He grinned. "I'd say so. I nearly got whiplash when you started pulling off your clothes. I figured it would be slow going and then wham, everything changed. What happened, anyway?"

"The more I saw of your chest, the more I wanted to interact with your naked body. Then I sort of kissed your shoulder while I was taking off your shirt and that started the lust attack."

"That was a defining moment for me, too. I almost grabbed you."

"That would have been okay."

"I didn't know that."

"Keep it in mind for next time." She moved her hands back to his butt and squeezed. "You can grab me anytime you get the urge."

His eyebrows lifted. "Anytime?"

"When we're alone."

"Thought there'd be an addendum to that statement." His expression grew thoughtful. "I suppose we need to talk about how things will be when we're around other people."

"Do you want to talk about it now?"

"Not really."

"Good. Me, either. It can wait." She gazed up at him. "What do you want to do?"

His smile was slow and sensual. "I thought you'd never ask."

"So soon? Don't you need time to—"

"Yes, ma'am, I surely do. But there are plenty of ways to occupy ourselves until then."

_18_

Paradise. Quinn didn't have a better word to describe lying in bed with Kendra while she allowed him to acquaint himself with the wonders of her body.

Stretched out on his side and propped on his forearm, he stroked her breasts, cupping first one and teasing the nipple until it sat up and took notice, then switching to the other. "So pretty."

"So happy."

"Hope so." He flicked the one closest to him with his thumb. As it darkened and grew stiff, his cock stirred. Wouldn't be long, now.

Her breathing had been relaxed a while ago, but the more he played with her breasts, the quicker her breaths. "I didn't think they were this sensitive, but tonight..."

"I woke them up."

"Guess so."

"Let's see if they're really awake." Moving over her, he leaned down and closed his mouth over that burgundy tip. Now he knew the color as well as the taste, and the feel of the pebbled surface as he rolled it against his tongue.

She made a sound low in her throat and his cock twitched. As he began to suck, her breathing ramped up a bit more. What a joy to make love to this woman.

Lifting his mouth away from one moist breast, he settled in to enjoy the other one while sliding his hand between her damp thighs. She gave him access and that gladdened his heart. So easy to slide his fingers into her slick heat and give her pleasure.

Abandoning her quivering breast, he kissed his way down to her nest of curls and lower, urging her to open for him, breathing in the heady aroma of aroused woman as he slowly, almost casually, took possession of her most secret place.

And she trusted him enough to be vulnerable, to give in to the response he wrung from her with his mouth, his tongue and the gentle scrape of his teeth. She moaned, she writhed, she whimpered, and at last she came, clutching his head and swearing a blue streak. If he hadn't been otherwise occupied, he would have laughed.

She was still quivering from her climax when he slid into position and entered her with one smooth stroke. Spreading his palms on either side of her head, he gazed down at her flushed face and grinned. "You have the mouth of a sailor."

She sucked in a breath. "And you have the mouth of a devil. You turned me inside out."

"You blistered my ears."

"You had it coming. You have a wicked technique, Sawyer."

"And you loved every minute of it, McGavin."

"I did."

He initiated a slow, seductive rhythm. "How's this working for you?"

"It's nice." She gripped his shoulders. "But I'm tapped out. You won't get another orgasm from me, if that's what you're going for."

"Nah. This is all about me. You don't have to do much except lie there."

"After what you did, I feel compelled to contribute." She grasped his hips, and on the next down-stroke, she did a sly little rotation. His involuntary gasp must have tickled her because she smiled. "Like that?"

"Yes, ma'am."

"Then maybe I'll just do it some more."

In no time at all, he'd lost control of the situation. Her hip rotation had him struggling to keep from coming and his whole plan had been to give her one more climax. He'd figured that if he played it cool, the next one would sneak up on her.

Instead he was ready to boil over at any minute and she was calm and collected. Or maybe not. That gleam in her eyes...and the extra pressure of her fingertips digging into his shoulders...

Yep, there was that telltale squeeze on his cock. "Tapped out?"

She moistened her lips with the tip of her tongue. "Maybe not."

"I definitely think not."

"Just don't expect—" She clutched his shoulders and arched off the bed. "Hallelujah! Here I go again!"

As she gasped and swore, he pounded into her and followed her over the brink. Damn this was good!

No wonder his favorite place was *W-I-T-H-K-M*. He could get even more specific than that. His favorite place was right here, between her satin thighs, his cock buried deep. Given that, he might want to decline a turn with the Ouija board next time someone brought it out.

* * *

Quinn wasn't surprised that Kendra liked to cuddle after vigorous sex. If this had been a test to see whether they were sexually compatible, they'd passed with flying colors. By mutual agreement, they curled up together for a little catnap.

He didn't plan to sleep long and he was good at setting an internal alarm. Although she hadn't said anything, he doubted she'd want him to stay until morning in case one of her boys spotted him coming out of the ranch house. Long before dawn he'd be back in his cabin and nobody would be the wiser.

When he woke up and saw the pale light of dawn filtering through the pine branches outside her bedroom window, he cussed softly to himself. His internal alarm had failed for the first time in years.

She was still zonked. What now? He hated waking her, but they needed to discuss this. He wasn't about to sneak out, hoping for the best, without asking how she wanted to handle it. Her kids, her decision.

Combing her hair back from her cheek, he dropped a kiss on her warm skin. Too bad he couldn't make that a prelude to an intimate caress. His cock would happily go along with that program. He hadn't experienced morning wood in a while. Inconvenient, but kind of nice that she inspired that in him.

She mumbled something and slept on. He put his mouth close to her ear. "Kendra, wake up."

She sat up very fast. If he hadn't reacted, she would have bashed him in the face. "What?" Confusion clouded her eyes. "What are you…" Her gaze sharpened and pink tinged her cheeks. "Oh." Then she glanced over at the window. "Oh!"

"My fault. I intended to sleep for an hour or so and head back to the cabin. But—"

"Cody's probably down at the barn. Maybe Zane, too. Normally I'm there by now."

"I'm really sorry."

"Not your responsibility. I should have set an alarm."

"How do you want to handle this?"

She ran her hands through her hair. "I'm thinking."

"I could just get dressed and walk to the cabin. They might be in the barn. It could be a non-issue."

"It might be a non-issue even if they saw you."

"I suppose, but they still might be startled if I come strolling out of your house."

"Or not. Deidre got me aside in the kitchen last night. While we fetched the pencils, they came up with a plan to calm my boys' fears. And maybe convince them they don't need to go into protective mode."

"How would they do that?"

"Faith would talk with Cody, Mandy would talk with Zane, Nicole would talk with Bryce and so on."

"Huh." He scrubbed a hand over his face and encountered the stiff bristle of his beard. "What were they planning to say?"

"That you weren't a threat to the status quo. We're just…having fun. You have your life and I have mine. Stuff like that. Mostly what you and I discussed last night."

"It's a good idea. I should talk to Roxanne, too. She moved here partly to be out on her own. She needs to know that dear old dad won't suddenly be living here."

"Right."

"I'll also have a discussion with my boys at some point."

"Would you need to? Aren't all your kids used to you dating?"

"Uh, yeah, but—" How to explain the difference? "I think it was obvious I wasn't…strongly attached."

She studied him. "You were just having fun?"

"Not this much fun." Maybe he shouldn't have said that, but it had popped out. The discussion was getting tricky.

"Hm."

"It's late." He climbed out of bed. "We'd better come up with our game plan, whatever it's going to be."

Her gaze traveled over him. "You're a hell of a handsome guy, Quinn."

"You're a hell of a beautiful woman, Kendra. I would love to spend the rest of the day in bed with you, but that's not in the cards."

"Have you ever spent a whole day in bed with someone?"

"No, ma'am. Have you?"

"No. Never even thought of it. But I'm thinking about it, now."

"We don't live that kind of life. Neither of us has the luxury of an entire day to do nothing but amuse each other."

"I guess not." She smiled. "Maybe we wouldn't make it through a whole day. Maybe we'd get bored."

"Do you think so?"

"No."

"Me, either."

She took a deep breath, making her breasts quiver invitingly. "Here's what I think we should do."

"Say to hell with everything and fly to Tahiti?"

She gave him a long look as if she might be imagining it.

He was, and he'd never had that kind of fantasy in his life. But to be alone with her, somewhere warm, without responsibilities...to have the freedom to eat, sleep and make love any time of the day or night...yeah, he could go for that.

"Let's take a quick shower, get dressed, and walk down to the barn together. We'll talk to them about this. Get it out in the open."

He nodded. "Good plan."

"If Faith and Mandy have laid the groundwork, it should be fairly easy. If they haven't, it's even more important that we not sneak around as if we've done something wrong."

"Which we haven't." He glanced at the rumpled bed and the lovely woman he'd shared it with. "Just the opposite. This feels more right than anything I've done in a long, long time."

19

Kendra sent Quinn down the hall to the bathroom her boys used when they'd lived at home. He chose to make the trip naked while carrying his bundle of clothes under his arm.

She leaned in the doorway and shamelessly watched his progress. What a great butt. "There's a package of disposable razors in the cabinet under the sink," she called after him.

"Thanks." He turned and walked backwards as he kept talking. "I need to get kiss-worthy again." Clearly he didn't give a damn that he was giving her a full-frontal show.

"Sounds good to me." Everything about him sounded good to her. His nonchalance about being naked was catching. They were alone in the house, so why not stand in her bedroom doorway wearing nothing?

"Are you sure we can't shower together?" He grinned at her. "Saves water."

"No, it won't because we'll fool around in there. This will save time and water."

"Assuming you go jump in the shower instead of standing there ogling me."

"I'm just making sure you know where you're going, which you clearly don't. You just passed up the bathroom."

"Because I'm ogling you."

"Okay, okay. Meet you in the living room in ten minutes." She turned and dashed into the master bath. Yikes. Her hair was sticking out in all directions but she sure looked happy.

She took the fastest shower in history, singing *Girls Just Want to Have Fun* at the top of her lungs. Dressing in record time, she quickly damp-dried her hair and made it into the living room in nine minutes, flat.

Quinn was waiting for her, his hair still wet and a tiny piece of toilet paper stuck to his jaw where he'd shaved too quickly and nicked himself. He'd put on the denim jacket he'd left hanging on the coat tree but left it unbuttoned. He held his hat in one hand.

His smile was a mile wide when she walked in. "Damn, lady. How do you do that?"

"What?"

"Look wholesome and sexy at the same time."

"I do?"

"Yes, ma'am." He gestured toward her. "Jacket, blouse, jeans, boots, no makeup. You're even wearing a baseball cap, for crying out loud. Can't get more wholesome than that. And I'm developing a woody."

"Because of what we've been doing."

"Nope. You've affected me like this from day one. It's worse, now, or better, whichever way

I choose to look at it. But I've wanted you from the get-go."

Her body tightened. "Same here."

"So even though my face is as smooth as a baby's butt, I'm not going to kiss you. That was my plan, but I can't take a chance I'll get carried away."

"That *we'll* get carried away. I'm in the same fix as you, buddy. That trip to Tahiti sounds really good right now."

"We'd freak out our kids."

"I know. We're not doing it, but it's fun to think about." She took a deep breath. "Ready?"

"Ready if you are." He walked over and opened the front door. "After you."

She stepped out on the porch. A breeze cooled her cheeks as she checked out the activity down by the barn. Zane's truck was there and the barn door was open. Then Zane came out and gazed up at the house.

She waved and he lifted his arm as if to wave back. Then he paused and lowered his arm.

Quinn's hand gripped her shoulder. "He just saw me come up behind you," he murmured. "He's waiting for us. Let's go."

This moment had been easier in her head. Zane nudged back his hat and stood in front of the open barn door, feet braced apart, thumbs hooked in his belt loops. Ian used to take that stance when he had something weighty to think about.

She didn't want to cause Zane, or any of her sons, anxiety. She didn't want to be a problem they had to work out. By accepting Quinn into her life—into her bed, to be more specific—she might have done that.

Cody's voice drifted from inside the barn. Zane turned and said something back before facing the house again. Then Cody came out and took a position next to Zane, copying his stance.

She was too nervous to smile at that, but it was cute, all the same. High noon. Except they weren't gunning for her. They loved her and she loved them. Change was hard.

When she and Quinn were about ten yards away, she called out *good morning* and smiled. Zane and Cody responded in kind but neither of them returned her smile. *Ah, my sweet boys. It will be okay.*

Eventually she was close enough to pause and say something. "This may be a little awkward for both of you."

Zane nodded. "Yes, ma'am."

"But Faith talked to me about it last night," Cody said, "and I'm okay with it. I shouldn't speak for Zane."

"I'm—" Zane stopped to clear his throat. "I'm okay with it, too. It's just...different."

"I understand. But I want you to know this doesn't change anything."

"Sure it does, Mom." Zane regarded her steadily. "You've never had a guy in your life before. This is a change. There's no getting around that." He glanced at Quinn. "Nothing against you, but—"

"What your mother means is that I don't plan to disrupt anything. I have my ranch in Spokane and running that takes up the bulk of my time. Kendra and I will see each other when we can, but it's not like I'll be hanging out here on a regular basis."

"That's what Faith said, too." Cody frowned. "And I don't get it. Seems like if you enjoy being with someone you'd want to be around them a lot."

"Exactly." Zane adjusted the fit of his hat. "This whole deal makes no sense to me, either."

She wasn't surprised. "Quinn and I are coming at our relationship from a different place than we would have if we'd met when we were younger. He's built his life in Spokane and I've built mine in Eagles Nest, so—"

"You can't ever be together?" Cody gazed at them in confusion. "How is that a good thing?"

"It's our compromise." She didn't expect him to understand. "Bottom line, I'm never leaving Wild Creek Ranch."

"Good." He heaved a sigh. "That's good."

"Like Quinn said, we'll see each other when we can."

"How often?" Cody still looked confused on that point.

She glanced at Quinn. "We haven't talked about that. But it's a long trip, so—"

"Maybe every couple of months," Quinn said. "We have to see how things go."

"Every couple of *months*? Won't you miss each other?"

Zane gave his brother a warning glance. "That's not our business. Or our problem."

"I know, but if it turns out they really miss each other and she decides to spend a lot of time in Spokane, then *that's* our problem."

"I promise that won't happen."

"I promise, too," Quinn said. "I won't take her away from here. I'll make the trip down."

She blinked. "You will?"

"Yes."

"But that doesn't seem fair."

"Let him do that, Mom," Cody said. "He's got that cool motorcycle. I'm sure he enjoys riding it. Besides, Roxanne's here, so he's got another reason to come to town. You'd only have him up there, so logically he should—"

Jim's truck pulled in next to Zane's and Zane lowered his voice. "Does Jim know about this?"

"I'm sure Deidre filled him in," Kendra said.

Cody leaned toward her. "But he couldn't know that Quinn spent—"

"He doesn't need to know that," Zane said. Then he raised his voice. "Hi, Jim! Think it'll rain?"

"Weather report says not 'till tonight." Jim ambled toward them. "Howdy, Quinn. Deidre told me you took part in the Ouija board shenanigans last night. She was impressed."

Quinn laughed. "It was interesting."

"You stuffed birdseed bags *and* messed with the Ouija board?" Cody's eyebrows almost disappeared under his hat.

"Sure, why not?"

"You wouldn't catch me sitting down at that board. I don't want anybody poking around in my subconscious." He glanced at Zane. "Did you ever fool with that thing?"

"Not me." A shrill whinny issued from the depths of the barn. "That would be Winston. Unless we want him to organize a revolt, we'd better finish up in there."

"Quinn and I will take the new barn," Kendra said.

Zane met her gaze and nodded. "Yes, ma'am." Then he turned his attention to Jim. "I've sorted the tack and put aside everything that needs repairing before the trail ride Saturday."

"Excellent. I'll get right on it this morning."

The trail ride. How had she managed to forget that she was scheduled to go out with Zane tomorrow, not to mention making the lunches for the group of six who'd reserved a spot?

Zane glanced at her. "Are you still available for Saturday or do you want Cody to go?"

"Of course I'm available." She wanted to say something more to Zane and Cody, but with Jim there she couldn't close out the conversation the way she would have liked. "Guess we'd better get a move on. See you all later."

Quinn walked beside her as they headed for the second barn. "I forgot that you do trail rides every weekend."

"You have no reason to remember. It's a little scary that I forgot, though."

"You did? I couldn't tell from your reaction."

"I hope Zane couldn't tell, either. I think he was testing me by offering to put Cody in my spot."

"No reason to. It's not like I expect you to spend the day with me. I need to track down a fuel tank for my bike."

"Any more leads?"

"Maybe. I have a couple of phone messages I haven't listened to yet."

"Gee, I wonder why."

"It's a mystery named Kendra McGavin. But even assuming I score a fuel tank today, I won't be leaving until tomorrow at the earliest. Is anything going on tonight?"

"Like what?"

"Family gatherings, bachelorette parties, sleepovers with your Whine and Cheese—"

"Nothing's going on."

"Then you and I could have the evening to ourselves?"

The heat that she'd kept on low during the conversation with her sons ramped up several degrees. "As far as I know. What do you have in mind?"

His chuckle was soft and intimate.

"That's not an answer."

"Yes, it is." He glanced at her. "I'll leave you to fill in the blanks."

20

Quinn shared breakfast with Kendra and Jim again. This morning he handled it better and so did she, evidently. She didn't drop anything. The promise of spending an entire night in her bed kept his frustration level down, too. He couldn't kiss her now, but he would kiss the hell out of her later.

His phone messages yielded two more potential fuel tanks and he borrowed Kendra's truck for the day to go check them out. He made the Bozeman appointment for mid-morning and the Billings one for mid-afternoon. That left him time to take his daughter to lunch.

He chose the diner because sitting in a cozy booth to discuss his relationship with Kendra seemed more private than a table at the GG. Bryce might be working the Friday lunch shift and he'd rather not chance having any of Kendra's sons accidentally overhear any of the conversation.

Not that Quinn planned to say anything different from what was being circulated by the women at last night's party or what he'd told Zane and Cody. But Roxanne knew him better than those folks. If she asked him honest questions he'd give honest answers that might not perfectly match the story being told about this romance.

They settled across from each other at a booth by the window. Roxanne had requested it. "I love this particular spot," she said. "It's the one Michael and I ask for every time we come in here for breakfast."

"You come here even though you live over a bakery?" What a treat to have private time with his daughter. She'd pulled her hair into a ponytail and wore no makeup. In her worn jeans and faded t-shirt, she could pass for sixteen.

"I tried to survive on a breakfast of baked goodies and coffee. It didn't work out well. I need protein."

"You didn't used to think so. You told me a balanced diet was a candy bar in one hand and a can of soda in the other."

"Because I was a little smartass."

"A lovable little smartass." He paused so they could each give their order to the server. Then he leaned back in his seat and considered how to begin.

"This is about Kendra, isn't it?"

He smiled. "Yes."

"You've been interested for a while."

"Ever since I met her."

"I'm not surprised. She's great." She fiddled with her silverware. "Is it serious?"

"Um…" He didn't know how to answer. "Define serious."

"Committed."

"I won't be dating anyone else, so I guess that's committed."

"But you've never dated more than one person at a time. At least not that I know of."

"You're right. I haven't."

"So what's different about Kendra?"

Everything. "She's fun."

"Well, that's good."

"And devoted to her family."

"Also good."

"And strong."

Roxanne smiled at that. "I assume you're not talking about her muscles."

"No, but she's strong that way, too. There's nothing wimpy about that woman."

She put down the fork she'd been messing with and leaned toward him, keeping her voice down. "Dad, are you in love with her?"

He blinked. "In love? Oh, I wouldn't go that—"

"Because you sound like it. And you look like it. And you've dated women before and never felt the need to take me to lunch and explain yourself."

"That's true, but this is a different situation." In love? That couldn't be right. Roxanne was in love, so she probably imagined he was, too.

"How is it different?"

"Kendra happens to live in the same town you've chosen. And now that you and Michael are engaged, there's a good chance you're here for the duration."

"And your point is?"

"I'll be coming down to visit Kendra, but I won't be moving here. I just wanted you to know that."

"Oh. I hadn't gotten that far in my thinking. I guess you and Kendra do have a logistical problem." She looked puzzled. "Isn't it a little early to make that decision, though?"

"Not really. She doesn't want to substantially change her circumstances, which she likes just fine as they are."

"How about you?"

"I have a great life. Pete and I make a good team and the ranch is doing well."

"So how are you and Kendra going to work this out?"

"I'll visit."

"Will she go up there?"

"Probably not. As Cody pointed out this morning, I have two reasons to come to Eagles Nest. She'd only have one to come up to Spokane."

She smiled. "Then I should be seeing a lot more of you. That's cool."

"Maybe not a *lot* more. That wouldn't be fair to Pete."

"Hm. That doesn't sound like—" She glanced up as their food arrived. "Yay. I'm starving."

That made him chuckle. "Got lost in a project, did you?"

"I did. Between my work and spending time with Michael, I forget to eat."

"I'm honored that you took the time to meet me and I'm glad it involves food."

"Of course I wanted to meet you. I've been dying to know how things were going out at the ranch with Kendra, especially after you shaved off your mustache. That was a huge tell, Dad."

"So it seems." He tucked into his food. "Did you know why Ingrid recommended the 'stache?"

"Not until yesterday, when everything came to light. Are you upset with her?"

"How can I be? She was trying to get Kendra and me together, which I wanted anyway."

"She'll be relieved to hear that you're okay with how things worked out."

"I should go talk to her." He took a sip of his coffee. "I'm embarrassed by how easily she appealed to my ego, though. A little hint that I'd look good with a mustache and I grew one, like a damned peacock spreading his tail feathers."

She grinned. "If the tail feathers fit…"

"You don't have to agree with me, you know." He regarded her with affection. "You really are a little smartass."

"That's my job. My brothers suck at it, especially Wes and Pete. Gage is a halfway decent smartass, but he can't hold a candle to me." She paused, her fork in midair. "Do any of them know about this new development?"

"Not yet." He lifted his eyebrows. "Unless you've texted Wes?"

"You know, normally I would have, but I've been so busy with my own stuff I haven't."

"If you wouldn't mind holding off, I'd like to explain this to him and Pete in person after I get back. Gage will just get a phone call since he's on the road, but—"

"Didn't you just say your visits down here would be about the same as before?"

"Pretty much."

"Then why tell them anything? You've been making trips to deliver your art, so they won't think anything of you driving down here every month or two."

"I suppose."

"Dad, you're missing the obvious. There's a reason you want to tell us about Kendra when you've never felt the need with anyone else you've dated."

He lowered his voice. "Look, I'm not in love with her."

"Then there's no reason to say anything to my brothers. Or me, for that matter. If nothing will change, then what difference does it make to us?"

"You have a point." He glanced at the food rapidly disappearing from her plate. "Want dessert?"

"You know it."

"Good. Me, too." He hailed their server.

"By the way, will the fuel tank you saw this morning work for Cassandra?"

"Unfortunately not, but maybe the one I'm looking at this afternoon will do the trick."

"Hope so."

"Me, too." But not really. Fixing the bike meant leaving Kendra. Now that he'd established that he wouldn't be back for at least a month and perhaps longer, he was in no hurry to ride away from Wild Creek Ranch.

He didn't mention Kendra again for the rest of the meal, though. Roxanne had made an excellent argument for dropping the subject.

Kendra had been obligated to inform her sons that life would go on as before because they'd had a front row seat for this developing romance. Logically they'd wonder if it would impact them and they deserved to know that it wouldn't. But if Kendra would never travel to Spokane, then his boys didn't have to know the whole story.

* * *

The second fuel tank wasn't right, either. Or it could be that Quinn had become extremely picky because not finding it paid benefits. In any case, the trip to Billings allowed him to shop for some things he might not have found in Eagles Nest.

A party store carried everything he needed for decorating. Next he stopped at a liquor store. Kendra might have the right booze but he'd rather bring it in than use up her stash.

He had to double back to find a supermarket big enough to carry what he wanted. The deli counter was well-stocked on a Friday afternoon. He wasn't the only one looking for party food.

Mission accomplished, he pointed the truck in the direction of Eagles Nest. If he hustled, he might get to the ranch while Kendra was giving a lesson. His idea didn't have to be a complete surprise, but he wouldn't mind if he could set up a few things in advance.

When he drove in, Kendra was perched on the railing while a rider circled the ring on the black mare named Licorice. He'd like to head down there and watch, but first he had work to do.

He made a fast trip to his cabin for his sketch pad and pencils. Then he smuggled everything into her bedroom without anyone taking notice. She'd tidied up since he'd left the room early this morning. The bed was carefully made. He wouldn't be surprised if she'd put on fresh sheets.

Decorating didn't take very long. The concept was hokey as hell, but this was a woman who'd danced in a bear suit. She'd like it. After depositing the liquor in the kitchen and the perishables in the fridge, he hung up her truck keys.

He'd debated moving his things into her bedroom and finally decided what the heck, might as well. He didn't have much and he accomplished it quickly. At last he walked down to the corral.

Faith and Jim were having a discussion over by the old barn. They both waved and Quinn waved back.

"Any luck finding a fuel tank?" Faith called out.

"Not today! Maybe tomorrow!"

Kendra glanced over her shoulder. "Hey, there."

"Hey, yourself." He climbed up and took a seat on the rail beside her. "How's it going?"

"Good. Sorry about the fuel tank."

He smiled. "Are you?"

"No."

"Me, either."

"Got any more leads?"

"One. Sounds promising. I'll check it out tomorrow. I had lunch with Roxanne."

"Oh? How'd that go?"

"Interesting. I'll tell you about it later."

"Okay." She raised her voice. "Shorten up the reins a bit, Katherine. You want to keep light contact with her mouth."

The girl, who looked to be in her early teens, did as Kendra directed. "She knows there's a man here. It's making her jumpy."

"Yes, and she needs to get over that."

"Licorice doesn't like men?"

"Not much. She gets skittish."

"Guess I haven't spent enough time near her stall to notice. Want me to leave?"

"Not unless she gets really unruly. Her response is more deeply ingrained than I thought. It's been more than a year and she still reacts, especially when she's carrying a rider."

The mare began to prance and toss her head.

"Keep a steady leg on her, Katherine."

"I'm trying." The mare kept fussing.

Kendra hopped into the corral. "Bring her to a halt. I'm coming over there."

"Listen," Quinn said. "I can leave. I don't have to—"

"No, stay. I want to try something." She walked over to the mare. Taking hold of the bridle she looked up at Katherine. "I'm going to lead you around the corral for a couple of laps. We're going to pass by Mr. Sawyer. I want you to keep talking to Licorice. Stroke her neck, tell her you love her."

"I do love her. I just wish she'd get over this. My dad can't get close to her and I know he feels bad about it."

"He probably does." Kendra led the mare toward Quinn while Katherine murmured to the horse and scratched under her mane.

Quinn sat very still. The horse clearly didn't care for him. Her nostrils flared and a rim of white showed around her dark eyes.

Kendra walked past, circled the corral and walked past again. The mare seemed slightly less agitated the second time.

"Okay, Quinn," Kendra said as she went past. "Let's see what happens if you climb down when we're on the other side of the corral, and then walk beside me for a time or two."

"Got it." He ended up making quite a few circuits with them before Kendra called a halt.

"That was helpful." She smiled at him. "She was definitely getting calmer. Thank you."

"Glad to do it. I'll open the gate for you ladies."

Katherine called out her thanks as she rode through.

Kendra followed, but turned back to him. "Meet you up at the house?"

"You bet." He couldn't wait to show her what he'd planned for tonight.

21

Kendra had prepared herself for the news that Quinn had found a new tank and would be installing it tomorrow. Instead he'd be on the hunt again tomorrow and would be around for sure on Saturday night. It was like the adult version of landing a very cool date for the prom.

Chances were good he'd be here on Sunday night, too. His presence at the family gathering could be interesting, but hey, bring it on. Now that their relationship was out in the open, she welcomed the chance to see how he functioned in that setting. It wouldn't intimidate him. When it came to socializing, the man had skills.

She walked back to the barn with Katherine and talked with the girl while she groomed her horse and put away the mare's tack. Katherine agreed they'd made progress today with Quinn's help. Then her mom arrived to drive her home. Katherine's dad didn't come anymore and her mom didn't stay for the lessons very often. She'd clearly lost patience with Licorice.

Kendra understood. Maybe her brainstorm of having Quinn walk the corral with them would desensitize the mare over time. She'd ask Jim or one of her boys to help with the next lesson, although they'd also lost patience after months of effort. Katherine and Kendra were the only two members of Team Licorice.

Too bad Quinn wouldn't be available to help. His energy had been exactly right, possibly because he hadn't built up any frustration or resentment toward the mare. Licorice might have sensed that.

But Quinn would be in Spokane for the next lesson. No point in dwelling on that, though. He was here, now, and they had a little time before the horses had to be fed. She wanted to find out about his lunch with Roxanne and the promising fuel tank lead. Mostly she wanted to kiss him.

He wasn't in the living room when she walked in the front door. She took off her Raptor's Rise logo cap and left it on the coat tree. "Quinn, where are you?"

"Back here."

Tropical music featuring marimbas, steel guitars and bongos filled the air. She laughed as she started down the hall. "You'd better not be lying in there naked."

"Would that be so terrible?"

"Only because I can't make love to your gorgeous self now. We have horses to feed." The beat inspired her and she danced the last few feet down the hall and into the bedroom. "I like the music, though. What are you—" She stopped and stared at the scene he'd created.

Two inflatable, seven-foot palm trees stood at the foot of the bed. He'd draped several leis over the headboard and laid out two beach towels side-by-side on the quilt. In between sat a bamboo bed tray containing two empty stemmed cocktail glasses with little paper umbrellas propped inside.

Behind the tray he'd placed his sketchpad with a *Welcome to Tahiti* message lettered above a beach scene of sand, surf and palms. The music poured from his phone lying on the nightstand.

He stood to one side, grinning. Then he swept an arm toward the bed. "Welcome to my Tahitian getaway."

"I love it." She smiled back, and it was a little wobbly. Going straight into his arms, she gazed up into those warm gray eyes. "I love, love, love it."

"Knew you would. We can make the drinks after we feed the horses. I have stuff in the kitchen for pina coladas and I got a pineapple and some munchies that—"

She pressed her mouth to his, halting the flow of information. She got the message. He cared enough to do something sweet and funny, an inside joke the two of them could share, a fantasy they could create together.

His arms tightened as he deepened the kiss. As the rhythmic tune played in the background, he began to move subtly to the beat. She moved with him, winding her arms around his neck and molding her body to his.

Splaying his hands over her bottom, he held her close as he rotated his hips in time to the exotic music. Desire danced through her veins as her heart sang along...*yes, yes, yes, yes. You, you, you, you.*

The music ended and he slowly lifted his mouth from hers. His voice rumbled softly in the silence. "Later." He let her go and stepped back. "We have horses to feed."

She gazed into eyes filled with the same yearnings she was struggling to put aside. "I don't wanna."

He gave her a crooked smile. "Me, either, but the next generation is counting on us to behave like responsible adults."

"I was afraid you'd say something like that."

"Come on." He took her hand. "We can fake it for a little while. Then we'll come back here, drink pina coladas, and go back to acting like hormonal kids who just discovered sex." He grabbed his phone from the nightstand and led her out of the bedroom.

He continued to hold her hand on the way to the barn. Nice. He told her a little more about his lunch with Roxanne, who'd suggested he didn't have to broadcast their relationship to his sons. Roxanne's reasoning made sense, especially since Kendra wouldn't be going up to Spokane. Or meeting Gage and Pete.

Maybe she never would. That seemed a little strange since Quinn was getting to know her family. Oh, well. The situation wasn't perfect.

When she and Quinn walked into the barn, no one else had arrived to feed. She glanced at him. "What do you know? We beat the kids."

"I heard that," Cody called out as he and Faith came through the door. "You didn't beat us by much. We saw you walk in."

Holding hands. She glanced at her son. His smiling blue eyes bestowed a silent blessing. How sweet was that?

He pulled out his phone. "Faith and I got distracted looking at baby stuff and lost track of time. I found a mobile to hang over the crib. It's got little boots and hats hanging from it. So cute." He turned the phone so she could see.

She peered at the image. "Very cute. You'd better start a list of things you'd like to have. Eventually we'll throw you and Faith a baby shower and you'll need gift suggestions for people." Until a moment ago, she'd been grooving on tropical music and sexy kisses. Time to transition to baby showers and nursery decorations.

"I already ordered this."

"Cody, you might want to wait on buying—"

"I stopped him before he went hog wild," Faith said. "But he also found a bear wearing a Stetson, a fringed vest and boots. I couldn't talk him out of that, either."

"Yeah, Mom, you have to see this bear." He tapped the screen and held it up for her. "How could I resist?"

She laughed. "I can't imagine. You were a sucker for bears when you were little, too. I think your favorite one is up in the attic somewhere."

"I wondered about that. Maybe after we finish with the horses, I'll go up and poke around.

I'll bet there are some other things I've forgotten about that I can clean up and give to the baby."

Yikes. Her fault for opening her mouth. "I'm sure there are, but it could turn out to be a big, dusty project. And once it gets dark, you just have that one lightbulb. You might want to wait until tomorrow."

Faith jumped into the discussion. "Yeah, let's wait until tomorrow. I want to go with you, and I don't feel like diving into some major deal tonight. I'd rather relax and put my feet up."

Thank you, Faith. Kendra gave her a quick glance and she managed a sly wink in Kendra's direction. Smart cookie.

"Okay, we can do it tomorrow. I'm just so excited about this baby. Zane keeps saying *I hope you know what you've gotten yourself into. They're a lot of work.* But I can't wait."

"Speaking of Zane," Faith said, "he called us a bit ago. He has a raptor rescue in progress so he won't be here to feed. But he said to tell you the problem should be under control by morning so he'll be on hand for the trail ride."

"Who's backup if he can't make it?" From babies to trail riding strategy. Goodbye, Tahitian fantasy, at least for now.

"I am," Cody said. "No worries. If Zane's tied up, I'll switch with him and let him take Sunday."

"Okay, good." She glanced at Faith. "I didn't even think to ask this on Thursday, but what did Doc Pulaski recommend when it comes to riding during your pregnancy?"

"She left it up to me, although I might have to take a break until the morning sickness is over. She also warned me about bladder issues on the long trail rides, but I personally think—"

"I can vouch that it's no fun going on a trail ride once that baby starts pressing on your bladder. I've had that start as early as three months. Let's plan on light duty during this first pregnancy, okay?"

"Thanks, Mom." Cody looked relieved. "I tried to convince Faith we can manage the trail rides without her for now. We have you, me, Zane and Jim. But she—"

"I just know summer is the busiest time around here," Faith said. "I don't want to let everyone down."

"Don't give it another thought. If necessary, we'll hire someone temporarily." Kendra turned to Cody. "Let's start looking for a good candidate in case we decide to do that."

"I'm all for it. And maybe for next summer, too. Faith says one of us can take the baby on the trail in some sort of cradleboard thingy, but I'm not so sure about that, either."

Faith lifted her chin. "That's what my dad did with me when I was little."

He glanced at her. "I know, but—"

"We'll cross that bridge when we get to it," Kendra said. "In the meantime, we have some hungry horses. Do you two want to take the new barn again?"

Cody nodded. "Sure." He looked at Quinn. "Forgot to ask. What's up with the bike? Faith said you're still minus a workable fuel tank."

"I'm checking out a good prospect tomorrow. The guy sent me pictures and it appears to be perfect."

"Where is he located?"

"Dillon. Easy trip. If I go first thing in the morning and the fuel tank is as represented, I might have the bike running by tomorrow night."

"Let me know when you're back," Faith said, "so I can watch."

Quinn smiled. "If you're available, I'll let you help with the work."

"Hell, yeah, I'll be available." Then she looked at Cody. "Whoops."

"That's okay. We've got almost seven months. We'll get there."

Kendra was mystified. "Get where?"

"Faith and I promised each other we'd clean up our language before the baby's born."

"Hm. Good idea. Guess I should do the same." But she'd delay that program until after Quinn left because she was prone to swearing during...oh, but he'd be coming back, so what then? Maybe she could learn to limit her salty language to times she was in bed with him...

"Mom?"

She blinked. "I'm sorry. Did you ask me something?"

"I asked what you want to be called."

"Called for what?"

"You know—grandma, granny, nana, mimsy—"

"Mimsy?"

He shrugged. "It was one of the suggestions online."

"I haven't heard that one. You know what, son? That little chickie-poo isn't even born yet, much less talking. We can let the name thing happen organically." Or she'd invent something. Cute but not too cute.

"Okay, but the article warned against leaving it to chance. Kids come up with strange ones. One poor lady was saddled with Boobsie."

"Oh, dear." She ignored Quinn's muffled snort of laughter.

"But if we start calling you something you like," Cody said, "then the baby will pick it up, too."

"Kendra's right, though." Faith looped her arm through Cody's. "We can worry about that later. Let's go feed the horses."

"I just thought—"

"Come on, Daddy-o." She tugged on his arm.

He laughed. "Now that name I like." He glanced at Kendra and Quinn. "See you both tomorrow."

"See you then." Kendra gave them a big smile. After they left, she walked to the door and leaned out to make sure they were well on their way to the new barn. Faith would likely see to it, though.

"What're you up to, lady?" Quinn's arm circled her waist.

Turning, she grabbed him by the front of his shirt. "Kiss me."

"Now? Aren't we supposed to—"

"Uh-huh. Right after you rocket me out of the grandma zone."

22

Quinn was as eager to get the feeding done as Kendra, especially after the way she'd kissed him when the kids had left the barn. He didn't make conversation while they worked and neither did she. Hay flakes were delivered with brisk efficiency and the job was finished in record time.

"You know, we don't have to make the pina coladas first," he said as they walked quickly back to the house.

"Yes, we do. I'm so touched by the trouble you took to set up our evening."

"I promise you'll be touched if we go straight to bed."

"We're not going straight to bed. We're going to make our umbrella drinks, fix some munchies and take them into the bedroom. I want that music back on and—"

"Our clothes off?"

"That's a given."

He smiled. "How far you've come in less than twenty-four hours, Kendra McGavin."

"I can't help it if you've got such a great body that I want to ogle you as much as possible."

"Backatcha, lady. Just so you know, while we were tossing hay flakes into the feeders, I was picturing the fun it would be to get naked and have an actual roll in the hay."

"It would be very, very prickly."

"I didn't mean literally rolling in it. I'd put a blanket down."

"Are you suggesting that we might have sex in the barn in the future, Mr. Sawyer?"

"I'm saying it's on the list. We'll take this one adventure at a time. Assuming we can wrangle the necessary privacy."

"No kidding. I could have kicked myself for mentioning to Cody that his bear's likely in the attic."

"You recovered nicely."

"Faith helped. Cody's oblivious."

"Yeah, well, that's natural. He'd rather not think about us doing stuff."

"I know." She grinned at him. "But I like thinking about it."

"You and me, both." One saucy comment and he was ready to grab her and try out a few Kama Sutra moves. He restrained himself. They had all night, after all. But his jeans pinched his privates as he climbed the porch steps and opened the door for her.

She went inside and headed straight for the kitchen. "Lock the door, please," she called over her shoulder.

"Lock it? I thought you never—"

"I don't, but Cody was ready to come in and sort through his things in the attic. Any one of my boys could take a similar notion and barrel into the house without thinking, especially if they've blocked out the possibility that we're doing anything in here."

He twisted the deadlock and followed her into the kitchen. "Don't they have keys?"

"Yes, but locking the door would be enough of a signal that they'd hesitate to use the key. That's the moment they might remember that tonight isn't the greatest time to come in unannounced." She lifted her blender out of a cupboard and set it on the counter.

"They're used to doing that?" He opened the fridge and took out the containers of food.

"Sure." She plugged in the blender and pulled a cutting board out of another cupboard. "I'll bet your kids are, too."

"I suppose they are, now that you mention it." He was seriously distracted. The door was locked and they were alone. Why weren't they kissing yet? Oh, right. She wanted to organize the food and drinks first. "We'll need to heat the food."

"What'd you get?" She came over to investigate and her arm brushed his.

She was in kissing range, but he restrained himself. "Some things on skewers, some dumpling-type deals and egg rolls. Shouldn't take long to warm up. Oh, and I got sweet and sour dipping sauce." He popped the top on the take-out boxes.

"Looks perfect." She walked away, rummaged in another cupboard, and came back with a cookie sheet and a pair of tongs. "Here you go. I'll start on the pineapple."

"Thanks." He transferred everything to the cookie sheet, put it in the oven and set the timer on his phone. Then he brought up the pina colada recipe and held the screen so she could see it, too. "Didn't know if you have a recipe."

"Somewhere, but since you have one handy, let's use that."

"Measuring cup?"

"Cupboard above the sink." She sliced the pineapple lengthwise, cutting through the top and laying out the two halves. "Then you don't lock your door, either?"

"Nope." Watching her create the pineapple boat was addictive. He forced himself to concentrate on his part of the operation and opened the rum. "There'd really be no reason to lock up, unless..." Unless she came to visit. He'd nixed that, though, hadn't he? Was that for her sake? Or for his, so he wouldn't have to deal with potential awkwardness with his sons?

Maybe a little of both, but mostly the decision would benefit him. He measured the rum and dumped it into the blender. "I just realized the setup we agreed to is unfair to you."

She stopped slicing and looked at him. "What makes you say that?"

"If I come down here all the time, you're the one who takes the heat."

"It's not that bad. The boys are getting used to the idea."

"Except I'm doing what I've always done, conducting my private life out of sight of my kids. Whereas you have to explain yourself to your sons and worry that one of them might stumble upon us making love."

She smiled. "You're worth it."

"Thank you for that, but—"

"Quinn, neither of us planned for this to happen. It turns out we're dealing with my family, not yours, but you didn't set it up that way on purpose. If anything, I'm the instigator. I invited you out here."

"But I'm the one who arbitrarily decided that I'd be visiting you and not the other way around."

"Which is logical. Roxanne's here, too."

"Would you like to come to Spokane?"

"Of course I would if we had only ourselves to consider. Seeing your ranch would be fun. Getting a peek at your studio would be exciting."

"Then you should come. I want you to. I'm proud of my ranch, and you could meet—"

She shook her head.

"Why not?"

"I've told my boys nothing's going to change. If I go up there and meet your family, it'll look like a next step, an escalation."

Who cares? But he didn't say it out loud because he knew the answer. She cared.

She'd laid the ground rules before they'd made love. No husband and no live-in boyfriend. Their relationship must not be allowed to disturb the status quo. Any sign that it might would signal the end.

He certainly didn't want that. "I see your point. I don't like the idea that you can't just come up there, but I get it."

"Good." She glanced at the blender. "How're the pina coladas coming along?"

"Your bartender got sidetracked, but he's on the job, now." He added cream of coconut, coconut milk and pineapple juice to the rum. "Some ice and some of that fresh pineapple and we're ready to create this sucker."

"How many servings does it make?"

"Four."

"That sounds about right." She'd scooped out both halves and mounded the pineapple chunks into one half.

"The pineapple looks festive."

"Does it make you think of Tahiti?"

"Absolutely."

"Me, too." She spooned several chunks into the blender. "Think the food's warm enough?"

Time to get this party started. "Depends on how hot you want it."

She picked up her cue. "I want it hot." Plucking a chunk of pineapple from the mound in front of her, she turned, her eyes heavy-lidded as she sashayed over to him. "Want some of this?" She slowly brushed the pineapple back and forth over his mouth.

"Uh-huh." He bracketed her hips, snugged her up against his crotch and held her gaze while she fed him the pineapple. His bad boy rose to the occasion.

"Oh, my goodness, my fingers are *so* sticky."

"Allow me." Grasping her hand, he took his time licking pineapple juice from her fingers.

Her breathing changed. "Thank you," she murmured. "Want more?"

"Depends on what we're talking about." He circled her palm with the tip of his tongue.

Her eyes darkened. "What are you talking about, cowboy?"

"Not pineapple." As he lowered his head, aiming for her saucy mouth, his phone let out the annoying beep he'd set for his timer.

Her laughter was low and seductive as she wiggled out of his embrace. "I want it hot, but I don't want it burned."

"Picky, picky, picky."

"You've got that right." Snatching up a couple of potholders, she took the cookie sheet out of the oven. "These all look great. Might as well start the blender."

"I need to fetch the glasses from the bedroom. Be right back." He took his phone, called up the Polynesian music he'd found, and left it on the nightstand. He grabbed a couple of the leis, put one on and looped the other one over his arm before lifting the tray with the glasses on it and going back to the kitchen.

She'd finished transferring the food to a platter. "Done." She turned around. "Now we— Quinn! You've been lei-ed."

"In one sense, but I'm holding out hope for the other kind." He crossed to her and slipped the second lei over her head. "Now so have you." He captured her face in both hands and gave her an open-mouthed kiss. He couldn't seem to stop, either. She tasted too much like heaven.

Evidently she had more brain cells working than he did, because she drew back and gulped in air. "The food's getting cold."

He knew that. He just hadn't been able to make himself care about anything but her tempting mouth. "Here's an idea. Take the food into the bedroom. Then I might manage to fix the drinks without needing to kiss you some more."

"I'll do that." She backed away from him, removed the glasses from the tray and put the platter of food on it. Then she grabbed napkins from a holder and took off.

After adding ice to the concoction in the blender, he had his finger on the switch when something, likely his guardian angel, made him glance at the counter. The lid was lying there. He shoved it on and flicked the switch. What an unholy mess that would have made.

Had he ever been this bonkers over a woman? Well, yes, more than thirty years ago, when the solution for such powerful feelings had been simple. Marry the girl. It sure as hell wasn't simple this time.

23

Kendra set the tray on the floor temporarily while she tore off her clothes. Once upon a time she'd had a black bikini. Was it still in the bottom of her drawer?

She dug around. Yes! Pulling it out, she wiggled into it. The bottom was a little tight, but she got into it. The top was borderline indecent, but since Quinn would be the only one who'd ever see her wearing it, no problem.

Propping pillows against the headboard, she decided to leave the tray on the floor for now. She could do a better job of lounging seductively on the bed if she didn't have to worry about dumping the tray.

She'd barely made it into position when Quinn walked through the door, an umbrella drink in each hand.

He sucked in a breath. Let it out slowly. Muttered an earthy swear word.

She ran a finger over the swell of her breasts that threatened to pop out any second. "You like?"

"I like." His voice was gravelly. "And guaranteed I'm gonna slop these drinks everywhere."

"Try putting them down slowly on the nightstand."

He followed her suggestion and managed to avoid spilling a single drop. Leaning against the wall, he tugged off his boots while continuing to stare at her. Then he started toward the bed.

"Hang on, there, cowboy. You're overdressed."

"If I get naked, there will be no eating or drinking. That's a promise."

Teasing this man was more fun than she'd ever imagined. "Then maybe you could just take off your shirt."

"Good idea. My jeans can function as a chastity belt." Snaps popped as he wrenched open his shirt, revealing the broad expanse of his lightly furred chest.

She sighed. "That view never gets old. Are you sure you want to leave on—"

"I'm sure." He ditched the shirt.

"Okay." She patted the beach towel next to her. "Come on down, big boy."

"Where's the tray of food?"

"On the floor beside me. I'll put it over my lap as extra insurance while we eat."

"Ah, sweet torture."

"Is it too much?"

"Nah. It's fun." He climbed in and settled against the stack of pillows. "Didn't factor in a black bikini, though."

"Last minute inspiration."

His attention returned to her cleavage. "I have to ask. Do you wear that out in—"

"In public? Years ago, I did. Deidre set up a girls' weekend in Bozeman at a hotel with a pool. We all got babysitters and bought bikinis. I was less...busty, then."

"You haven't worn it since?"

"No."

He swallowed. "Good, because you could cause a riot."

She laughed.

"God's truth, Kendra. I don't know how you can be sexier with it on than without, but you are."

"Just so you think so."

"There's no thought process going on in this brain. It's fried."

"Goodness. You need food and drink to revive you. Shall we try those pina coladas?"

"Good idea. Might cool me down." He handed her one with great care before picking up his.

Taking out the little umbrella, she raised her glass. "Here's to adventure."

"Here's to you. All the adventure I'll ever need." He touched his glass to hers and locked his gaze with hers as he drank.

She went still. All the adventure he'd ever need? What did that mean?

"Something wrong?"

"I—your toast..."

"Oh, that. Toasts are supposed to be dramatic, over the top." The intensity had disappeared from his expression and his eyes twinkled with amusement. "I was just kidding around."

"Oh." She took a drink. "That's a very good pina colada."

"Thanks. Need help with that tray?"

"I've got it." Years of developing her core strength through riding and mucking out stalls allowed her to lean over the bed and lift the tray to her lap without breaking a sweat.

But she almost fell out of her bikini top. She adjusted the material.

"I could help you with that, for sure."

"You mean help me out of it?"

"Actually, no. I'm becoming fond of that look."

She savored the husky timbre of his voice, one of the many joys of having a lover. She'd missed that. Positioning the tray over her thighs she handed him a couple of napkins. "Dive in."

"I love it when you talk dirty." He picked up a skewer and began eating.

"That's nothing. You should hear me swear."

"I have."

"I know. Just wanted to make sure you were paying attention." She dipped one of the puff pastries in the sweet and sour sauce.

"Always."

And she was basking in all that attention. "I'm wondering, after what Cody and Faith said, if I need to start watching my language."

"When?"

"Well, all the time." She ate the pastry and chose one of the skewers.

"That would be sad. I look forward to hearing you turn the air blue. That's how I know you're having a really good time." He snatched a chunk of pineapple and popped it in his mouth.

"So you're not offended?"

"I'm honored. You wouldn't let loose like that if you didn't trust me."

She glanced at him. "I do trust you."

"I trust you, too."

His easy smile tugged at her heart. There was more than sexy fun going on between them and she didn't know how to change that dynamic. Or even if she wanted to.

Sometimes, when she caught him looking at her with tenderness as well as desire, she wanted nothing more than to snuggle close and revel in the warmth and security of his strong arms. Instead of simply making love, she wanted to be loved.

Not that she didn't have plenty of love in her life. Her sons and her friends cherished her as much as she did them.

But that wasn't quite the same as being adored by a man who shared her bed on a regular basis. Sex with Quinn was amazing, but the closeness and camaraderie were precious, too.

"There's more pina colada in the kitchen. I'll go get it."

To her surprise, her glass was empty. That would explain the delicious languor suffusing her body. She focused on the inflatable palm trees at the foot of the bed and could almost imagine them waving in the breeze, especially with the marimbas and bongos playing in the background.

The whir of the blender told her that he was remixing their drinks. He'd probably put the glass pitcher in the fridge to keep it chilled, too. Thoughtful behavior. Quinn behavior.

He returned with the frothy mixture and executed a decent cha-cha step before refilling both their glasses.

"Nice moves, Sawyer."

He waggled his eyebrows at her. "I'm way better at the horizontal mambo. Just sayin'."

"Talented *and* modest. How did I get so lucky?"

"I have a thing for women in bear suits." He set the pitcher on the nightstand. "That's it unless we want to make another batch."

"This'll do it for me." She waited until he'd climbed in before taking a sip. "I'm feeling very pampered."

"Good. I wanted this to be like a mini-vacation for you."

"For you, too, I hope. I'll bet you don't take many."

"How about zero?"

"I'm not surprised." She munched on pineapple.

"Because you don't take them, either?"

"Nope."

"We really are two peas in a pod."

"But I love my life."

He nodded. "Me, too, but..." He glanced over at her. "Goofing around with you is a blast."

"And you know what? Your little cha-cha step inspired me." She put her drink on her nightstand and took hold of the tray. "Ready to ditch this?"

"Absolutely." His eyes lit up. "Are you ready to—"

"Dance! Let's dance to this great music. If we were on vacation we'd do that, right?"

He laughed and put down his glass. "We definitely would."

"Meet you by the twin palms." She danced around the bed and chuckled as he did the same. Then she cupped her hand over one ear as she continued moving to the syncopated beat. "I can hear the ocean!"

"Good thing I got a room right on the beach. And wow, look at that view."

"Can you see the water from here?"

"No, but I can see your ta-tas struggling to break free. No better view than that."

She started giggling. "Should I set them free?"

"I wouldn't object."

"Then prepare yourself for a topless cha-cha."

"Can a guy ever be prepared for—whoa!" He gulped and his steps slowed. "Hey, that's seriously...sexy..."

"Hope so." She gave an extra shimmy and twirled around, arms over her head. "I—oof!" She ran into the solid wall of his chest.

"Sorry. Can't stand it." Scooping her into his arms, he carried her to the bed and toppled onto it while he kissed her...everywhere.

The bottom part of her bikini was gone in no time. Then he simply undid his jeans and shoved them to his knees before entering her and beginning to thrust. The wild, spontaneous thrill of it spiraled through her, tightening the coil of excitement until she was panting with anticipation, reaching for...oh, yes, that, and that and *that*.

The first spasm of her climax brought a hoarse cry of triumph from Quinn. He drove in faster and gasped for air. "C'mon, Kendra. Let me hear you."

Rising to meet him, she let go, coming and shouting out every colorful word she knew.

"That's it, that's *it*." Plunging deep, he shuddered in her arms, his harsh breathing nearly drowning out the music.

Slowly he lowered his forehead to her shoulder and let out a ragged sigh. "You make me crazy."

She stroked his sweaty back. "You make me come."

"I know. I love doing that. It's...wonderful."

"Ready to take off your jeans and stay awhile?"

His warm chuckle tickled her skin. "What's the world coming to when a guy can't even wait to take off his pants?"

"My fault for being so damn sexy."

"That's the truth. Please promise me you'll do that again sometime."

"I might. Better keep those tropical tunes handy."

"Don't worry. I will." Lifting his head, he placed a gentle kiss on her mouth. "But I'm thinking our island musicians are about to go on break. Okay with you?"

"Sure. But give them a big tip."

"I will." Easing away from her, he rolled to his back and rid himself of his jeans. Then he picked up his phone and silenced the marimbas and bongos before turning on his side to face her. "Hi, there."

"Hi, yourself." She traced the line of his jaw where his beard was starting to grow. "This has been great. The decorations, the food, the music...thank you."

"With all the kids' birthday parties I've organized over the years, I've had a lot of practice."

"And because I'm a kid at heart, I loved it."

"Yeah, I am, too." Wrapping an arm around her waist, he drew her against him. "That's why I have a motorcycle."

"Which brought us together."

"Or rather, it brought us together faster. I always planned we'd get to this point eventually."

"Oh, did you, now?"

"You didn't know that I had designs on you?"

"I wasn't sure. Clearly you wanted to be friends, but since you live in Spokane, I figured that might be all you wanted."

"Wrong-o." He stroked the curve of her hip. "I wasn't going to let a little seven-hour drive stop me."

"I see. Did you have it planned beyond this point?"

"No. I wasn't willing to let the drive stop *me*. It could have stopped you, though. Fortunately, it hasn't."

"Which is your fault because you're so damn sexy. And since you'll be coming down once a month or so to bring your work to the GG, our plan makes sense. It doesn't change either of our routines hardly at all."

"I've only stayed two nights each time, though."

"Only two?"

"I didn't want to impose on Roxanne." He leaned closer, his mouth almost touching hers. "But I could stay a few extra nights if someone offered me a warm bed."

"And a Tahitian vacation?" She snuggled against him and pressed against his thickening cock.

"Sign me up." He nibbled on her lower lip. "I had no idea I'd enjoy Tahiti this much."

"Ready to enjoy it some more?"

"Yes, ma'am, I sure am." And he captured her mouth.

24

Quinn focused on making sweet love to Kendra. And when they were both well and truly sated, he remembered to set his phone alarm before they went to sleep. She had a trail ride in the morning.

Spending the night hadn't been part of his dating pattern over the years, but it was the most natural thing in the world with Kendra. He treasured being allowed to hold her as she drifted off to sleep in his arms. Enjoying this pleasure a few nights out of every month would be meager rations, but that might be all they could manage, at least for now. Better than nothing, right?

The next morning, he showered in the bathroom down the hall again. After the usual feeding routine, he and Kendra grabbed a quick breakfast. Then he helped her pack lunches for the trail riders.

Getting the horses tacked up was an all-hands-on-deck situation and Quinn assisted there, too. Zane was available for the ride, so Cody didn't have to be pressed into service.

Quinn's involvement gave him a greater appreciation for the trail riding operation and the work involved for Kendra. She hadn't slept a whole lot last night, but she was a trouper. She'd been perky and smiling as she'd waved goodbye.

After he saw them off, he climbed into her truck and drove to Dillon. And damn it all, he missed her. He didn't like her going off in one direction and him in another. He'd done it yesterday, so what was wrong with him today?

He was getting in deeper, that's what. He'd better watch out. If she sensed it, she might send him packing, no matter how much she liked him.

Road construction on the way to Dillon turned what should have been a relatively short trip into a much longer one. He hadn't expected crews to be out on a Saturday. Maybe they were taking advantage of the good weather to get the repairs done before the summer tourist season was in full swing.

In any case, he was late getting to Dillon and the old cowboy with the fuel tank was a talker. Quinn bought the tank, which was exactly what he needed, and stayed for lunch because the guy clearly wanted the company.

It was the least Quinn could do for a fellow Harley owner who'd come up with the right part for his bike. And a spare helmet. Quinn bought that, too.

Lunch lasted a while, though, and Quinn didn't get back to the ranch until late afternoon. He had several reasons to install the new tank immediately and only one to postpone the job until tomorrow. Postponing would give him one more night with Kendra.

If he wanted to get this craving under control, he'd be wise to finish the repair now and leave in the morning. He parked the truck up by the house, pulled out his phone and texted Faith that he'd be starting the repair in about fifteen minutes if she was able to meet him at the barn.

Then he hopped down from the cab and headed for the ranch house. He was way too eager to see Kendra, but by leaving tomorrow, he could start to put this arrangement into perspective.

They'd be long-distance lovers and he'd better be grateful for that because she wasn't offering anything more. If he couldn't be satisfied with that scenario, he had the option of rejecting it. No one was forcing him to accept her terms.

But when he walked into the house and she came out of the kitchen looking flushed and happy, he was willing to accept any terms she dictated. "Hey, there."

She came straight into his arms and hugged him tight. "Hey, there."

"Where is everybody?"

"We just finished feeding and Zane's gone home to Mandy. Cody's up in the A-frame looking at baby stuff with Faith."

"Then maybe she won't want to come down and help me with the bike. I ended up coming back later than I expected."

"You found a fuel tank?"

"Afraid so."

"No, no, that's a good thing." She gazed up at him. "Probably a very good thing. I missed you today."

His heart turned over. "I missed you, too."

"But we need to be grownups about this. Missing each other when we're apart is the price we pay for keeping our lives stable."

Holding her warm body brought him stability, too, and he sure did like doing that. "If I install the tank now and all goes well, I can leave in the morning."

She took a deep breath. "Then you should aim for that."

"Anything going on tonight?"

"Not a thing but hanging with you. I'm warming up some stew for our dinner."

He'd considering taking her out, but if she'd already started something, he'd selfishly rather keep her all to himself tonight. "That sounds great, but unless you're starving, I'd like to fix the bike and take you for a short ride. I picked up an extra helmet and a pair of gloves today."

"I'd love that."

"Then I'll change into my old smelly clothes and get 'er done." Giving her a quick kiss, he let her go and walked quickly back to her bedroom. The house was starting to feel like home. That might not be so good, either.

When he returned to the living room, she was in the kitchen so he just called out to her rather than going in there. "I'll be back as soon as I can."

She didn't come out. "Great! See you then."

Yeah, this was becoming way too familiar and domestic. He'd take her for a ride on his bike, make love to her again tonight, and leave for

Spokane tomorrow. Might as well get used to the leaving part. That was the way it had to be.

* * *

The rumble of a motorcycle alerted Kendra that Quinn had pulled up outside. Moments later he walked through the door. "Fuel tank's perfect."

"Good. Did Faith come down to help you?"

He smiled. "Sure did. She's quite a mechanic. And she wants a bike like mine."

"Then I predict someday she'll have one. Ready to go?"

"Give me five minutes to change out of these clothes. I don't want you hanging onto me when I smell of gas."

"Want some help?"

He laughed. "I'll take a rain check. See you in a few." His long strides carried him quickly down the hall to her bedroom.

His footsteps on the wood floor, his voice, his laughter, his touch—she'd miss all of it when he drove away in the morning. Chances were good he wouldn't be back for another four or five weeks. *Weeks.* But she'd help set the parameters, so she'd jolly well better be able to handle them.

Well, she would, that's all. He couldn't come more often without piling extra work on his son and she'd made the choice not to visit him in Spokane.

It wasn't ideal, but it was that or nothing. In any case, anticipating future sadness and ignoring current pleasures made no sense. When

Quinn started back down the hall, she unhooked her denim jacket from the coat tree. "I assume I'll need this."

"You will, although I'll block the wind so it shouldn't be as cold for you."

"I can't wait. I've never ridden on a motorcycle before."

He came to an abrupt halt. "Never?"

"It's a small town. Growing up I didn't know anybody who had one. It's still a small town and I still don't know anybody with a motorcycle. Except you."

"I had no idea I had a virgin biker on my hands."

"Is that a problem?"

"On the contrary. It's a privilege and a responsibility."

She grinned. "It's getting deep in here."

"I'm serious. If I do this right and you have a positive experience, there's a chance you'll become a champion of the sport. If I screw it up, you'll tell your friends that you never want to get on that damned machine again and you might convince them not to try it, either."

"So much pressure!"

"No worries." He smiled and grabbed his jacket off the coat tree. "I'm not going to screw it up. You'll love it. You have all the makings of a biker chick."

"How do you figure?"

"You're gutsy."

"Thank you."

"You love being outdoors."

"Yep."

"And you have a great ass."

She laughed. "Thanks. I'm so ready to plant my great ass on your bike so you can take my gutsy, outdoorsy self for a ride."

His gray eyes twinkled. "Right this way."

She walked out the door ahead of him and gave a little twitch to her hips.

"Did I mention sexy as hell?"

"No."

"Add it to the list." He took her hand and laced his fingers through hers as they started down the flagstone walkway. His bike sat at the end of it, gleaming in the light from the porch.

"What about the dirt road? Will that be tough on Cassandra?"

"She's used to it. My ranch road's dirt, too."

The road she'd never drive on. The ranch she'd never see. He'd learned so much about her by staying here. She wouldn't get that chance. Her choices were starting to feel like bars caging her in.

"Ever worn a motorcycle helmet?"

"Nope."

"Then I'll help you put it on." He unhooked one of the two secured to the bike. "The guy who had the fuel tank just broke up with his girlfriend and she didn't want her helmet or her gloves. If they fit you, I'll leave it all here for the next time I ride my bike down."

"Weren't you taking a chance, buying a helmet without me there?"

"A little. But after making love to you I know the shape of your head."

"You're kidding."

"Not at all. Tilt your head toward me. That's good."

"While we made love, you were measuring me for a helmet?"

He chuckled. "No, ma'am. I was having the time of my life. But the info registered, anyway. Whenever I cradled your head in my hands. I just naturally—"

"Is this a motorcycle geek thing?"

"Probably." He crouched down and fastened the chin strap. "How does it feel?"

"Like I'm ready to rocket into space."

"Are you uncomfortable? Are your ears squished?"

"I'm perfectly comfortable. I just feel like Buzz Lightyear."

"You don't look like Buzz Lightyear."

"What do I look like?"

"A Harley biker chick." He strapped on his helmet and handed her the gloves. Then he gave her a quick course in the art of being a passenger on a motorcycle. "The best thing is to hold tight to me and follow the movements of my body."

"Oh, baby."

"No, really. If you do that you'll be safer and—"

"More turned on?"

"I have no control over that."

"Me, either. Fire her up."

He laughed and shook his head. "I have a feeling this will be a very memorable ride." Straddling the bike, he started the motor and motioned her to climb on.

Adrenaline pumping, she settled behind him, wrapped her arms around his waist and pressed herself firmly against his strong back.

His voice rose above the grumble of the engine. "All set?"

"Let her rip!"

He took off slowly and she tightened her hold. She'd underestimated the erotic potential of riding behind a virile motorcycle man. Quinn Sawyer on a red 1983 Harley...*booya.*

He took the dirt road at a leisurely pace, allowing her to look up at the stars. Spectacular. Two minutes into this ride and she was already a fan. She breathed in the earthy tang of spring grass mingled with the now-familiar scent of Quinn. She could identify him blindfolded.

During his instructions, he'd explained that if she looked over his left shoulder, she could keep her body aligned with his. She didn't need to do that. Instinctively she moved when he moved.

When he reached the paved two-lane, he picked up speed. The air rushed past and her heart raced in time with the spinning wheels. Glorious! As he took each curve, she dipped and swayed with him as if they were dancing.

The road was nearly deserted. A couple of trucks passed them on their way into town. Most people were settled in for the evening, leaving this stretch of road for her first-ever magical motorcycle ride.

On the outskirts of town, Quinn slowed and executed a gradual U-turn. Homeward bound. She didn't want the ride to end and yet she couldn't wait to tell him how much she'd loved it.

He'd brightened her life in so many ways and this was icing on the cake. No wonder he'd bought this bike and thank goodness he'd chosen to ride it down here. Had Trevor been psychic when he'd imagined her perfect man coming into town on a motorcycle?

Like before, Quinn took it easy on the ranch road. Not as smooth a ride as the highway provided, but she had time to appreciate her surroundings more. Her beautiful ranch. How ironic that the place she loved was one of the reasons she couldn't be with the man she....

Oh, hell. Damn it, no! Please don't let it be... But it was. Dear God, she loved him. Horrible news. The worst. The sharp pain started in her gut and moved into every cell in her body. What had she done?

When she loved, she didn't mess around. She didn't make logical compromises—a little time together, a lot of time apart. The distance separating her from her beloved morphed into miles of barbed wire, endless stretches of parched desert, a rocky terrain filled with broken glass.

As a young bride, she'd barely survived Ian's tours of duty. She'd struggled to frame them as a noble sacrifice because he was serving his country. Hadn't worked. Missing him had become a visceral, gnawing ache that filled every waking moment and spread misery through her dreams. Torture.

She would never sentence herself to that kind of half-life again.

25

Best bike ride ever. Quinn had expected fun. He hadn't expected transformational. He could have kept going for hours, but he didn't want to overdo it on Kendra's first outing.

She might be hungry. Or turned on. He was, but not to the point that he'd need to drag her straight to the bedroom or go crazy. Not that she'd ever needed to be dragged.

After she'd conquered her anxiety that first time, she'd been all in. God, how he'd miss making love to her, miss talking and laughing with her, miss…her.

He pulled the bike up in front of the flagstone walk and waited until she swung down. After he turned off the engine, he nudged down the stand and climbed off.

She was struggling with her chin strap.

"I'll get it." He helped her off with her helmet and set it on the seat. "What did you think?"

"I loved it." But her voice sounded funny.

He took off his helmet and gloves before he glanced at her. "You're a great passenger."

"Thank you." She handed him the gloves she'd worn. Her expression was subdued, which didn't fit with her body language during the ride.

He'd swear she'd been transported by the experience, too. He didn't take the gloves. "Might as well keep them. And the helmet, too." He picked it up and gave it back to her.

She avoided looking at him as she accepted it and dropped the gloves inside.

Yeah, something was seriously wrong. "Kendra, what is it?"

She met his gaze at last. Before the ride her eyes had been filled with anticipation, happiness, excitement. Now...unreadable. "Would you please come inside and make love to me?"

"You know I will, and gladly, but—"

"Please don't ask me anything, okay? I just...need you."

He nodded. Leaving his helmet and gloves with the bike, he took her hand for the silent journey along the flagstone, up the porch steps and over to the door. His head buzzed with a million questions she didn't want him to ask. Maybe he didn't want to know the answers.

Inside he helped her off with her jacket and shrugged out of his. What a strange turnaround from the lighthearted woman she'd been earlier. Sliding his hand around her waist, he walked with her back to the bedroom where she'd left on a light as usual.

No tropical music tonight, though. They'd deflated the palm trees and put away the leis. Nothing remained of their happy little party. Just as well. The mood had completely shifted.

Cupping her face in both hands, he kissed her. Grasping his head, she kissed him back with an urgency that spoke of desperation. Then she backed away and began taking off her clothes. He got the message and started on his.

She finished first. Throwing back the covers, she stretched out on the snowy sheet and watched him as he shoved off his jeans and briefs. She murmured something he didn't catch.

"What?"

"You're perfect."

"Hardly."

"Perfect for me, then."

He took a deep breath. "That's great to hear." And confusing. Perfect for her was good, right?

He gazed into those blue eyes as he slipped in beside her. "You look so sad."

"Please make love to me, Quinn."

"I don't have to be asked twice." It was a lame excuse for a joke. The Kendra he was used to would have pointed out that clearly he did have to be asked twice because this was her second request.

But she said nothing, just reached up and stroked his cheek with a tenderness that made him catch his breath. What was going on?

Moving over her, he dropped soft kisses on her cheeks. When her eyelids fluttered closed, he brushed kisses there, too.

Her touch was light but thorough as she caressed his shoulders, his arms, his back. Almost as if she wanted to commit him to memory because...*no*. He refused to go down that dark and dismal path.

Instead he'd build a fire in her that would drive out whatever demons she was battling. He roamed the length of her warm body, stroking, nibbling and licking all those secret places that he'd learned could bring her to a fever pitch.

Gradually she began to respond. Her breathing changed first, then the pressure of her touch. At last she began to moan and thrash beneath him.

That was more like it. Capturing her mouth, he put everything he was reluctant to say into his kiss. He ravished her sweet lips until he was out of breath. Lifting his head, he sucked in air. "Tell me what you need."

Clutching his shoulders, she dug in with the tips of her fingers. "I need...please...I want..."

He moved between her thighs and plunged deep. Then he leaned down and put his mouth close to her ear as he drew back and drove home again. "This?"

"*Yes.*" She gasped the word and arched to meet his next thrust. And the next.

He settled into the rhythm that worked for them. He could gaze into her eyes as they changed color, watch the flush of an impending orgasm suffuse her skin.

"You're perfect, too." He changed the angle a little and she tightened around his cock. "Perfect for me."

The glow in her eyes intensified.

"I never thought I'd find...someone like you." She was close. He increased the pace.

"But...here you are." He bore down. "Come for me, sweet Kendra."

Faster now, and faster yet. She arched upward with a wail and her climax rolled over his cock as he continued to pump. Her orgasm triggered his and he claimed his release, adding his deep groan to her breathless cries. But she didn't swear.

His breathing slowed and he gave her part of his weight, just enough to let his chest nestle against her breasts. He kept his voice light. "What happened to the salty language?"

Her soft whimper was his first clue that he'd asked the wrong question. Then he glanced into her eyes. Uh-oh. Tears quivered there, ready to spill out. "Kendra? What's wrong, sweetheart?"

"I love you."

He stared at her, stunned. And elated. And some other emotions he didn't have the brain power to process yet.

"I'm sorry."

That snapped him out of his confusion. "Sorry? What's to be sorry about? That's wonderful!"

"No, it's not! It's terrible!" The tears spilled out from the corners of her beautiful eyes.

He was undone. He'd fight dragons to stop those tears. "How can it be terrible? Don't cry, please don't cry. We'll work it out. I'll fix this. Just tell me what—"

"It's not your fault. Well, it is, because you're so great. I should have resisted, but I didn't and now we have a huge mess." She pushed at his chest. "You need to move so I can get a tissue."

"Stay put. I'll bring the box." She loved him. How did he get so damn lucky? *She loved him.* How terrific was that? He returned to the bed with a renewed sense of purpose. "You love me?" He still couldn't believe it.

"Yes, damn it." She pushed herself to a sitting position and took the box of tissues he offered.

"Hey, it's okay. I love you, too." He climbed back into bed and sat facing her.

"You do?" She looked horrified. "That's even worse!"

"You're confusing the hell out of me. How can it be bad that we love each other?"

She blew her nose and gazed at him with such despair in her eyes that he reached for her. She scooted back. "I guess I need to explain."

"I guess you do." That little scuttle movement away from him hurt. She'd always wanted to come toward him, not back off.

She used up several more tissues as she talked about Ian and the pain of his absences while he was deployed. "I never got used to it." She blew her nose again. "That yo-yo of being with the man I loved and then not, and then with him again for a little while, and then he'd be gone again. Horrible."

He was getting the picture and it wasn't pretty.

She wadded up a tissue in her fist. "Maybe you'd be fine with it. Maybe being in love with me and only seeing me every month or so would work for you."

"I don't know. I've never tried an arrangement like that. But I'm willing to, because the alternative—"

"That's just it. I'm not willing to."

The bottom dropped out of his world. "We'll shorten the time to three weeks. Let's do that and see how it goes."

She shook her head and reached for another tissue. "I love you, Quinn."

"And I love you, Kendra. That's why—"

"I can't love you only a couple of nights every three or four weeks and call that a life. I just can't! It's too hard!"

"So you'd rather have nothing?"

"*Yes.*"

He sucked in a breath. Not much to say to that, was there? He gestured to the rumpled sheets. "Then why this?"

"I'm weak. I wanted to make love with you one more time because it's the most wonderful thing that's happened to me in—"

"Damn it, Kendra!" He grabbed her whether she wanted him to or not. "Can you hear yourself?" He gave her a little shake. "The most wonderful thing that's happened to you in years! That's what you were going to say, isn't it?"

"Yes."

"It's the most wonderful thing that's happened to me in years, too." He loosened his grip on her arms and rubbed them gently. "I can't believe you don't want to at least try this arrangement. If you hate it, then—"

"Then I'll be even more in love with you than I am now. I'll have tortured myself and made it even worse when the breakup comes." She took a shaky breath. "I never told Ian this, but if he'd chosen to stay in the military and make it his career, I was going to divorce him."

That was a conversation stopper.

"When this all started, I convinced myself that it could work because you'd only be a diversion, a fun, amusement park experience that I could look forward to every month or so, like a massage or a pedicure. But you've become way more than that."

"So have you."

"Then take it from me, Quinn. We're not the kind of people who can settle for scraps when we want the full meal. That's probably why we clicked. You might not have discovered how bad our solution was until you'd lived with it for a while. But when you did, you'd have wanted out, too."

His jaw tightened. "I can't imagine wanting to cut you out of my life."

"You're angry with me."

"Yes. Angry and frustrated and...in love with you."

"I'm sorry about that."

"Me, too." He left the bed and started putting on his clothes. "No, I'm not sorry, or I won't be when I get some distance from this. You've taught me that I'm still capable of...what we've had. The damnable part is that I know how rare this kind of connection can be. I don't expect to find it again."

There was nothing more to say. All his stuff was here, and it wasn't much. He gathered it up. His bike was out there waiting. He could text Roxanne from the road to let her know he'd left. "Goodbye, Kendra."

"Goodbye, Quinn."

He walked out of the house. Climbing on his bike had always felt liberating. Not tonight.

26

Kendra stayed where she was until the rumble of the motorcycle's engine faded into nothingness. Then she got dressed.

She'd made the right decision. The foreseeable future wouldn't be fun, but she'd saved herself a boatload of long-term pain. She'd saved Quinn future pain, too, although she didn't expect him to ever thank her for it.

The last time she'd lost the love of her life, she'd surrounded herself with her children. But each of those boys was happily communing with a woman who had become the love of his life. As it should be.

She could still surround herself with her children, though. She opened a bottle of wine, grabbed a bag of chips and took both into the living room. Then she built a fire, even though the mild weather didn't justify it. She needed a fire tonight.

So many photo albums. She made three trips carrying them to the couch. She'd been faithful about making albums, although she'd switched from individual prints to creating the albums online.

She started at the beginning, with her wedding album. She'd never told a soul that she'd contemplated divorcing Ian if he'd chosen the military over her. Quinn would keep her secret, though.

Adding that bit of information had been necessary, although Quinn still hadn't understood her decision and perhaps never would. Not surprising. He didn't have her experience.

She put aside the wedding album and picked up the next one. As imposing as Ryker was now, he'd been a cute baby with an adorable smile. She had more first-year pictures of Ryker than any of the other four and she'd heard about that. No amount of explanation had mollified the others.

Sipping her wine and munching on chips, she closed Ryker's album and opened the next one. Zane shared his album with the first shots of Trevor and Bryce. By the time Cody came along, she had no shots of him by himself. He was so beautiful that someone, usually one of her girlfriends, always wanted to hold him.

Then she came to the tough part, where Ian disappeared from the pictures. Did Quinn have photo albums like this? He might, but guys she'd known weren't as likely to create them.

He might not find solace by looking through them the way she did, though. If she had to guess how he'd get through this, she pictured him diving back into his art.

That would be a sharp reminder every time she walked into the GG and his work was hanging on the wall. She'd almost bought one of his large pieces even though it was pricey. Good thing she hadn't.

She stared into the fire and sipped her wine. He'd still show up in Eagles Nest from time to time. She might run into him. If that happened, she'd greet him as a good friend. He had been. One of the best.

Her phone chimed with its generic ring. Not a family member. Quinn? She'd never gotten around to assigning him a ring tone.

Heart racing, she put the albums aside and hurried into the kitchen where she'd left her phone. By the time she grabbed it, the caller had hung up. She checked the readout. It wasn't Quinn.

She took several deep breaths. He wouldn't call, but maybe she should assign him a ringtone anyway so she wouldn't panic every time her phone chimed.

Then it pinged with a message. She listened to it. *Hi, Kendra, it's Roxanne. Dad just left me a message that he's on his way home and he'd explain later. It's not like him to ride into the night like that. If you could please call me, I'd appreciate it. Thanks.*

He was riding all the way home tonight? What an idiot! She'd assumed he'd spend the night with Roxanne and go home in the morning. He wasn't seventeen anymore, damn it.

She called Roxanne. "Hi. I thought for sure he'd come and bunk with you for the night."

"And I thought he was still out at Wild Creek Ranch. What happened?"

"We...figured out that the long-distance thing wouldn't work for us."

"Did you guys have a fight?"

"Not exactly. Eventually I think he'll understand it's for the best, but right now—"

"He's upset."

"Yes, but I never expected him to do something this stupid. What's he thinking?"

"He's headed for his safe place, the Lazy S. I doubt he wants to talk about it and if he'd come here, he would have felt the need to explain."

"You're right. And now I wish...well, what's done is done. Did you text him back and tell him to stop at a motel along the way?"

"I did, but he won't. The best I can hope for is that he'll respond to my text when he makes a pit stop."

"How many of those will it take?" She had no concept of mileage for a bike.

"At least a couple. I can ask him to text me each time he stops, but he's not gonna want to. He'll tell me to go to sleep and not worry, that he'll text me when he's home."

"Did you call Wes?"

"I did. Told him to expect Dad around four in the morning. He'll pick up an hour going home. Wes will probably text him, too. Read him the riot act, most likely."

"Roxanne, I'm so sorry. If I'd had any clue he'd take off, I would have handled this differently."

"It's not your fault. To be honest, I saw this coming. When I had lunch with him, he had all the signs of being in love. He wouldn't have been able to handle the arrangement you guys came up with."

"I know." Her throat tightened. "Neither of us could have."

Roxanne sighed. "Talk about a no-win situation."

"I count it as a win."

"You do?"

"I don't regret a minute I spent with your dad." She swallowed. "He's a very special human being."

"Yeah," she said softly. "He is. Want me to text you when I hear from him?"

"Please, if you don't mind. I'll keep my phone handy. I need to know..."

"That he's safe. I understand. I'll keep you in the loop."

"Thank you, Roxanne. You're a pretty special human being, yourself."

"Thanks. I learned from the best. I'll be in touch."

Kendra disconnected, closed her eyes, and said a little prayer that Quinn would arrive home in one piece. It would be a very long night.

* * *

Quinn hadn't meant to worry anybody. When he stopped for gas and looked at his phone, he had texts from Roxanne, Wes and Pete. Roxanne must have called Wes and Wes had relayed the info to Pete.

At least they hadn't alerted Gage about this night ride of his, but clearly he was in deep shit with his kids. He sent them a joint text assuring them he wasn't tired at all and he was making good time.

Both were true. He'd always loved riding at night but hadn't done much of it recently. Maybe he'd known he'd catch grief for it. Evidently when a guy hit fifty he wasn't supposed to do things like this.

Cruising along on his bike made the years fall away, though. Hanging out with Kendra had the same effect, but love was blind, just like they said. He hadn't seen the cliff until he'd taken a swan dive over it.

Sad thing was, he got where she was coming from. If he could make it past his injured pride, he might eventually admit she was right to call a halt. He wanted her to be happy all the time, not just on select days of every month.

How ironic that he'd dated women in Spokane who could have handled the proposed arrangement just fine. He hadn't been a major player in their lives and vice versa. He hadn't fallen in love with any of them, though, had he?

On his second pit stop, he grabbed a cup of coffee and texted the kids again. If the roles had been reversed, he would have wanted that consideration from them. He hadn't anticipated that Roxanne would go into panic mode but maybe he should have.

Oh, hey, had she called Kendra? Damn, she might have. He texted Roxanne again to ask.

The reply was immediate. *Yes, and she's very concerned about you. I promised to keep her informed.*

Hell. He hadn't meant to worry her, either. This ride had been great for allowing him to process and clear his head, but it sucked for his loved ones. And Kendra was a loved one, even if she didn't want to be. Better text her, too.

He stared at the screen. They'd officially said goodbye. All very dramatic and final. Texting her was anticlimactic. But he was willing to bet she'd been up all night because of him.

Texting was the right thing to do. He sighed and began. *I'm two-thirds of the way home. Not tired. Don't worry.* He deleted the whole thing and started over. He had no business telling her not to worry.

Should be home in another hour or so. Roxanne said she'd talked to you. I'm sorry for causing everyone to worry. He hesitated. Decided to go for it and finished with *Love, Quinn.* Then he hit Send before he lost his nerve.

Swallowing the last of his coffee, he tucked his phone in his jacket pocket. It pinged with a return text as he walked out to his bike. He paused next to the Harley and opened the text.

Thank you for letting me know. Love, Kendra.

Her closing sucker-punched him, leaving him short of breath. He took a moment to get his bearings before strapping on his helmet. Even then, he didn't climb on the bike right away.

He was heading home on the assumption that once he got there, acceptance would set in. Distance would give him perspective and eventually he'd view his time with Kendra as a beautiful experience that wasn't meant to last.

Sounded good, didn't it? Maybe it would work out exactly like that. Then again, maybe he was feeding himself a line of BS. Maybe his life would never be the same.

Climbing on his bike, he started the engine and pulled out on the highway. The miles rolled away beneath his spinning wheels. *Love, Kendra, Love, Kendra, Love, Kendra.*

27

Quinn was home, safe and sound. Kendra read his text for the umpteenth time as her tight muscles began to relax. Evidently he'd figured out that Roxanne had called her and she'd be as concerned as his kids were about his late-night ride. Crazy man.

The text was so Quinn. *I'm home, putting my bike away and preparing myself for an ass-chewing from Wes and Pete. Love, Quinn*

She'd texted back that she was glad he'd made it. She'd signed hers with the L word, too. She'd figured if he had the courage to be open about how he felt, she could do no less. Just because they couldn't work this out didn't mean she'd stop loving him, just as he wouldn't stop loving her.

Although it was only four his time, it was five hers. She'd showered earlier to try and relax her tense muscles. It hadn't worked, but now she could pull on clothes and head down to the barn. Might as well get a jump on the day.

She'd made it halfway through the feeding routine when Cody showed up. She'd picked up a hay flake but put it down again. Cody would have questions.

"Hey, Mom!" He glanced around as he walked down the wooden aisle toward her. "Did Quinn leave already?"

"Actually, he left last night."

"Oh." He gazed at her, his cheerful smile fading. "That seems...abrupt."

"It was. But it's okay. We've both realized that we're not suited to a relationship where we see each other for a couple of days a month."

"I could have told you that."

"And I wouldn't have listened."

"I'm sorry, Mom." Nudging back his hat, he gave her a hug. "This sucks."

"It does, but you know what? Having Quinn around was fun while it lasted. And now I can concentrate on important stuff like your wedding and the baby. Speaking of that, how's Faith this morning?"

"Still barfing, poor woman. Evidently I hover too much, so she told me to go feed and leave her to upchuck in peace. That's why I'm here a little early. Not as early as you, though."

"You know me. Working in the barn is my therapy."

"Mine and Zane's, too. And speaking of the devil, here he comes. Hey, bro!"

"Hey, you two. Where's Quinn?"

"I'll let Mom fill you in. I'll get started on the new barn. Come on over when you're done here."

Zane nodded. "It's you and Jim for the trail ride today, right?"

"Yep."

"And a family dinner tonight?" Zane looked to her for confirmation.

"That's the plan. Six o'clock."

"Pot luck?"

"You know, we'd better do that. I haven't given much thought to groceries recently."

"No problem. Mandy and I will come up with something and Aunt Jo's always looking for an excuse to bake."

"Faith and I will bring our world-famous chicken," Cody said. "See you two later."

"Be there in a few!" Zane called before turning in her direction. "Are you okay?"

She took a deep breath. "Yes. And the situation with Quinn is...over."

"Over?" He frowned. "But you two seemed so happy."

"Like I told Cody, we wouldn't be so happy if we only saw each other once a month or so. Good thing we realized it before we got in any deeper."

"Huh." He rubbed the back of his neck. "So that's it? He won't be around anymore?"

"No, he won't." She ignored the sick feeling in the pit of her stomach. "It's for the best."

"I suppose. Although I was sort of getting used to the guy."

That made her smile. "Are you saying you'll miss him?"

"I wouldn't go that far." He studied her. "But you'll miss him. I can tell that."

"For a while. I'll get over it."

"Well, sure. You're a strong lady. You can handle anything."

"Not quite true, but thank you. I can handle most things, including this."

"It's just that while he was here you were so...smiley and stuff. I mean, you're always upbeat and cheerful, but he really made your eyes sparkle."

What to say to that?

"I mean, maybe this didn't work out, but what if someone else comes along, someone who lives in the area?"

I don't want someone else. "I guess anything's possible."

"That's all I'm saying. I think Quinn made all of us look at things a little differently."

"Good."

"Yeah, I think so."

"I have a favor to ask, though."

"Name it."

"I'd like you and Cody to spread the word before we all get together tonight. Never mind Aunt Jo. I'll talk to her this morning. But if you could let everyone else in the family know that the Quinn episode is over and I'd rather not discuss it, that would be a huge help."

"We can do that."

"Thanks. For the next week, I want the focus to be on Faith and Cody." She smiled. "And the munchkin."

"You've got it."

* * *

Jo opened the door of her condo, took one look at Kendra and folded her into a bear hug. "Oh, honey."

Kendra lost it. She'd stoically refused to cry after Quinn had ridden away, but lack of sleep and the warm understanding of her best friend stripped her of her defenses. Pacing the length of Jo's living room, she poured out her frustration and misery between sobs.

"Jo, the man's perfect! Magnificent lover, considerate friend, gorgeous body, and he happens to live in damned Spokane! Why does he have to live in stupid Spokane?"

Jo sat on the sofa and listened, making small noises of comfort as Kendra raged.

"And why does he have to be so wonderful?" She glared at Jo, who just shrugged and looked sympathetic, so she barreled on. "It's like finding the most beautiful pastry that you know is more delicious than anything you've ever tasted, and you can't have it!"

"I know. I'm sorry."

"I'm sorry, too! Zane thinks someone else will come along. Ha! There's not another man in the world like Quinn Sawyer." She choked out the words. "Nobody can kiss like that man. And I'll never kiss him again!"

She stomped and ranted for a little while longer, but eventually she ran out of steam. Coming to a halt, she faced Jo. "That's it." Her voice was nasally and hoarse. "I'm done. You got any cake?"

"Well, duh. Go in the bathroom and splash water on your face. I'll have it dished by the time you come back. I assume you want coffee."

She gave Jo a semblance of a smile. "Well, duh."

They sat in Jo's cute little dining nook, so different from the massive pine table and dining area she'd had in the house now owned by Zane and Mandy.

Kendra attacked the large slice of chocolate cake with a vengeance and asked for a second piece.

"Didn't you eat breakfast?"

"Didn't feel like it."

"Want me to scramble you some eggs?"

"No, thanks. Cake is exactly what I need." She finished off the second piece and sat back with a sigh. "Do you think chocolate cake could take the place of great sex?"

"No."

"You're supposed to say yes. Give me something to cling to." She gazed at Jo. "I've never had so much fun in bed. Not even with Ian."

"I believe you. Quinn's had more time to get really good at it."

"That's the damned truth." She groaned and buried her face in her hands.

"Are you sure you don't want to reconsider the once-a-month deal?"

She lifted her head and met Jo's gaze. "Don't think I haven't thought that myself. But no, I'm sure. The sex is good partly because we've fallen in love with each other. That plan would turn me into a whiny, needy bitch. I'd ruin everything."

"So what now?"

"I'll concentrate on Cody and Faith's wedding." She reached over and squeezed Jo's arm. "Thanks for letting me decompress. I really needed that."

"Yes, you did, and you're welcome."

"Will you tell the others about this for me?"

"Sure."

"Normally I'd suggest a meeting of the Whine and Cheese Club, but with all the last-minute details of the wedding to handle this week, I don't think there's time."

"The week after the wedding we'll call a meeting and get smashed."

"Good idea." She left her chair and poured herself another cup of coffee. "Want more?"

Jo held out her mug. "Hit me."

"You know what else was great about having Quinn around?" She sat at the table and cradled her coffee mug.

"He scratched your back?"

"Well, yes, he did that, and he's an excellent back scratcher. You know how some guys don't take direction well in that department?"

"I do know."

"Quinn goes right to the spot and keeps scratching until I ask him to stop."

"Then he's a prince among men."

"He is, but that wasn't the big thing I wanted to mention. What makes me love him all the more—he made me forget I'm about to become a grandma."

"Ah." Jo smiled. "That is a talent. If the Sacred Ouija Board is right, I'm going to be right behind you. That hit me kind of hard, too."

"We're not that old, right?"

"We might be old enough, but I don't feel grandmotherly."

"Me, either. Cody asked me to come up with a name I want to be called, like nana or something."

"Did you?"

"Not then. I told him we had plenty of time, but last night, while I was sweating out whether Quinn would make it home okay, I figured out what I want to be called."

"Which is?"

"Gramma Ken."

Jo started to laugh. "Gramma Ken! I love it. You'll confuse the hell out of people."

"I know. It'll be awesome."

"Oh, wait, I just thought of something. You'll be Gramma Ken, and if Mandy gets pregnant, I can be Gramma Jo."

"Excellent!" Kendra grinned and gave her a high-five. "This grandma gig is sounding better and better." She gave her friend a fond glance. "You're a great friend, Jo Fielding."

"Backatcha, Kendra McGavin. Think you'll live?"

"Yes, ma'am, thanks to you."

_28_

Typically, Quinn preferred to take his time with decisions. A lot more time if the issue was major, and this one was. But the urgency of the matter dictated a speedy resolution. His loved ones were involved and dilly-dallying wasn't fair to them.

It had been a busy week. A foal had been born on Wednesday and another of his mares could go into labor at any time. She hadn't yet, though, and Quinn needed to talk privately with Pete while they had a break in the action. On Friday, he suggested a late afternoon ride to evaluate forage in the pastures.

He saddled Banjo, a buckskin who'd earned his name because he was supposedly high-strung. He'd bought him for next-to-nothing ten years ago and had settled him down. Best saddle horse in his barn.

Pete tacked up Clifford, the big red roan Quinn had bought him for his sixteenth birthday. Pete and Clifford had been buddies ever since. Their personalities were similar, loyal to the core. They had some physical similarities, too, both big-boned and gentle.

To say Quinn was nervous about this conversation would be an understatement. So much depended on Pete's reaction. Quinn wouldn't allow Pete to dictate the course of events, but he wanted his eldest son to be happy.

They started at the far pasture and worked their way in. Pete typed notes on his phone regarding patches of healthy grass and areas of mud that needed to be tended. The more grass, the less supplemental feeding necessary. Quinn spent his time just looking. He loved the Lazy S. It was an important part of his past.

It was also the only home Pete had ever known. He had close friends here. He'd almost married a girl from Spokane, but that hadn't worked out. If it had, this discussion would have taken a much different direction.

Quinn asked Pete to hold up when they topped a little rise that gave them a view of the ranch buildings and the horses grazing in the spring-green pastures.

He leaned on his saddle horn. "I have something to discuss and I'm worried it'll rattle you." Gazing at his eldest son, he saw himself twenty years ago. The other three kids had taken after their mother, but Pete had the Sawyer genes.

He smiled as if enjoying a private joke. "Wes and I wondered when you'd bring up the subject of Kendra. We have a wager on it."

"Is that so?" Once upon a time he'd fancied himself a step or two ahead of his offspring. Now he was several steps behind. "Are you going to win?"

"I am. Wes was convinced you'd talk to one or both of us by Wednesday."

"We had the foaling on Wednesday."

"True, but I was betting that you wouldn't be ready by then, anyway. I said it would be today. And here we are out inspecting the pastures, which is a dead giveaway. Whenever you have something on your mind, you get me out here to evaluate the forage."

"Good God, am I that transparent?"

"Maybe not to everybody, but I've been around you more."

"Since you already know so much about this discussion we're about to have, why don't you tell me what I'm going to say?"

Pete laughed. "Before you start thinking I'm psychic, you should know something. While you were making your epic midnight ride, Roxanne, Wes and I were on a video chat comparing notes."

Quinn groaned. "I have no secrets."

"Sure you do. We don't know exactly what went on at Wild Creek Ranch, but—"

"Thank God for small favors."

"Roxanne's convinced that you're in love with Kendra."

"She's right."

"Have you been in love with any woman since Mom died?"

"No. Kendra's the first."

"That's what we all decided. Roxanne says Kendra's in love with you, too."

"Yes, I believe she is." Quinn had no control of the conversation whatsoever, but maybe that was okay.

"Roxanne also said Kendra's living on a ranch that she inherited from her folks, the ranch where she was born. Her roots run deep."

Quinn glanced at him. "I don't know where you're getting your intel, but it's excellent."

"All from Roxanne. She's our boots on the ground."

"My daughter the foot soldier." Quinn chuckled. "You still haven't told me what I'm going to say to you."

"It's not hard to figure out, Dad. Kendra's not leaving that ranch. If you want to be with her, you have to leave this one."

Quinn stared at him in amazement. "You said that so calmly, as if it wouldn't jackhammer the hell out of your life."

"It'll change my life, no question. I just need to decide how much. First off, I'd appreciate knowing your plans. Would you move in with her?"

"You flabbergast me, son. I only know one person who's more practical and straightforward than you, and that's me."

He smiled. "Where do you think I learned it?"

"Point taken. And the answer is no, I won't move in with her. She's made it clear she doesn't want a husband or a live-in boyfriend. I've investigated the possibilities and there's a little ranch across the main road that's for sale."

"Close, but not too close."

"Exactly."

"But not big enough for a horse breeding operation."

"No. It's a gentleman's ranch. I could take Banjo and maybe have another two or three, but that's it. Instead of horse breeding, I'd concentrate on my art."

"What about the Lazy S?"

"That's the sticking point. I'll need to sell it. I could sell it to you with a sweetheart deal, but—"

"That would leave you cash poor, Dad. I know the bottom line as well as you do. If you sell to me with a small amount down, which is all I can afford, you can't buy that gentleman's ranch."

"I still might be able to swing it. Or I could rent a house in town."

"A house in town? What about Banjo?"

"They have stables in Eagles Nest. Kendra owns one, in fact."

"You'd be miserable living in town."

"I'll be miserable if I can't be with Kendra."

"Nobody wants you to be miserable at all, Dad. We're going to sell this ranch. Let somebody else slave over it."

"What will you do?"

"Roxanne and I talked about it and she's excited having us move to Eagles Nest."

"Us?"

"Yep. Unless you hate the idea, I'll move to Eagles Nest with you. Me and Clifford, plus maybe another horse or two if there's room. We might need spare horses."

"You know I won't hate the idea. That would be great, but you'll be leaving your friends."

"I'll visit. They'll visit. Most of them are busy with wives and kids, anyway. We don't get together like we used to."

"I guess that's true, now that you mention it."

"It's partly because I'm so involved with the ranch. The Lazy S? I laugh every time I look at the sign out by the road. I haven't had a lazy minute in the past ten years. Have you?"

"Can't say I have." At least not while he was here. A pretend Tahiti getaway with Kendra was all he'd managed. "But I know you. There won't be enough to keep you busy on the place I'm considering."

"No problem. I'll get a job in Eagles Nest or one of the surrounding towns. Wrangle horses for someone else. Be an employee for a change."

"But this is your childhood home. And Wes's childhood home, and Roxanne's—"

"We're not kids anymore. And you're not getting any younger."

"Ouch."

"Sorry, but we've all talked about this and if you're in love for the first time since Mom died, that's a big deal. It takes precedence. You should go for it and we'll all support your quest."

"It's a quest, now, is it?"

"Roxanne likes that word. Anyway, I've never met Kendra but Wes has and Roxanne says she's terrific. They both think you'd be a fool if you didn't figure out some way to make it work with her."

"Wow. I guess I've been given my marching orders."

"Isn't that what you want to do?"

"Yes, damn it. That's exactly what I want to do, but I was worried that it would be a catastrophe for you kids."

"The only catastrophe would be you passing up a chance at happiness. Don't do it, Dad."

"Okay, Pete." He straightened in the saddle. "I won't."

29

The myriad details of Cody and Faith's wedding were Kendra's salvation. Faith had begged for a simple ceremony down by Wild Creek. Kendra understood the impulse. Both Cody and Faith had trekked around the West the previous summer taking videos of unspoiled vistas.

A ceremony down by the creek was appropriate, but it was far from simple. The guest list had been trimmed to forty but those forty folks still needed a place to sit. White wooden folding chairs had been rented, but nothing could be arranged until a couple of hours before the ceremony.

Even then a herd of deer or worse yet, elk, could romp through the area if it was left unattended. Kendra had nightmares of smashed chairs and trampled flowers. But she couldn't say no to Faith and Cody, whose image of the perfect wedding came straight from the heart.

She'd balked at staging the rehearsal out by the creek, though. Instead they'd held it last night in the front yard of the ranch house, followed by a rehearsal dinner around the fire pit.

Today, at wedding march time minus ninety minutes, the men were setting up the venue creek-side. They'd been blessed with good weather.

The wedding party of ten was large considering the small guest list, but Cody couldn't imagine getting married without all four brothers standing up there with him. He'd agonized over who to choose as his best man and had ended up giving all of them that designation.

Faith and her attendants were holed up in Faith and Cody's A-frame with Nicole supervising hair and makeup and Mandy helping everyone into the dresses she'd created. No doubt April had diffusers with an orange blossom scent going full blast and Olivia would be feeding everyone chocolate chip cookies.

Kendra was delighted they were up there and not in her house. She loved them all, but for sheer efficiency, she couldn't beat the Whine and Cheese Club. The reception would be around the fire pit, too, and without the help of her girlfriends, who'd been organizing parties for decades, she would never have managed both the rehearsal dinner and the reception.

The past few days had been wild, but she'd welcomed the chaos. Every minute spent dealing with wedding issues was a minute not obsessing over Quinn. Whenever she took a break from her duties, her traitorous brain switched to the Quinn channel and her equally traitorous heart followed.

Not much chance of that happening today, though. After she and her girlfriends were satisfied that the food was under control, they used her bedroom to change clothes. They'd no sooner returned to the living room than Abigail and Ingrid arrived with the wedding cake in a tall white box.

"It goes on the dining table," Kendra said. "But can we wait to take it out of the box until after the wedding? Faith is all about the big reveal."

"Except I'm dying of curiosity." Deidre walked over to the table.

"Faith already told me she wanted to keep it hidden until the reception. But she won't mind if I show you guys," Abigail said. "Wait'll you see how this box works. Trevor designed it for me and it's freaking amazing."

"Trevor?" Kendra hadn't heard about this. "But he's a carpenter."

"And this box is made of wood. That's why it takes both of us to carry it. It's heavier than cardboard but I can use it over and over."

"What a clever idea." Jo peered at the box as Abigail and Ingrid slid it carefully onto the table.

"The sides are tongue and groove. I can slide one up so you can see the cake and put it back down so the cake's hidden. When the time comes, I can remove all four sides, stow them and the top piece in my SUV, and the bottom of the box stays put until the cake's gone."

"That's brilliant," Kendra said. "How did Trev end up making you a cake box?"

"He came in the other day and we got to talking about the whole transporting nightmare and keeping the cake a secret." Abigail took off the top. "Next thing I know, he's back with this box. Because it's heavier than cardboard, it's less likely to slide or tip on the drive to the venue." She lifted one side to reveal the cake. "Ta-da!"

"Wow!" Kendra moved closer to examine the cake. "Great job! Faith and Cody will love this." Abigail had frosted the tiers alternating dark chocolate and milk chocolate. The milk chocolate tiers looked like tooled leather belts with silver buckles.

"If I didn't know better, I'd swear those belts were real." Deidre gazed admiringly at the cake. "I'd almost be willing to make a trip down the aisle just so I could have one of these."

"Calm yourself," Jo said. "If that's all you want out of the deal, we'll get Abigail to make you one."

"Which I absolutely would. You don't have to get married to order this cake."

Ingrid glanced around. "What did we do with the cake topper?"

"I left it in the car. Be right back."

Kendra stepped away so Christine and Judy could get a better view. As everyone continued to exclaim over the artistry of the cake, Ingrid moved closer to Kendra and lowered her voice. "I'm sorry."

"About what?"

"Quinn."

"Oh." She shrugged and managed to keep a smile on her face. "It wasn't meant to be."

Ingrid looked as if she might say something more, but Abigail returned with the topper, which kicked off another round of oohs and ahhs. The miniature scene depicted a bride leaning down from her horse to kiss her cowboy groom. Perfect choice for Faith and Cody.

"Uh-oh," Deidre said. "I hear the guys coming back. Better close up that sucker."

The cake was covered and the topper put away before the men arrived. Everyone except Luke headed back to the boys' old bedrooms to change.

Luke came over and gave Abigail a quick kiss. "You look terrific. How did Trevor's box work out?"

"Perfect."

"And the cake?"

Kendra answered for her. "She did an amazing job."

"Can't wait to see it. My folks and my sis should be here any minute. I'll be back as soon as I can." He hurried through the living room and down the hall where jokes and laughter were causing quite a ruckus.

Judy rolled her eyes. "Just like days of old."

"Yeah." Kendra smiled. "Music to my ears."

Shortly after that, Luke's family showed up. Luke's dad Warren was clearly in party mode. He was the funniest minister Kendra had ever met, but underneath all the kidding, he was very serious about the sanctity of a marriage. He'd had several meetings with Faith and Cody in the run-up to the wedding.

Soon Luke and Badger hurried out of a back bedroom putting on their Western-cut jackets on the way. They'd volunteered to escort guests to the venue.

"Would you look at that." Virginia, Luke's mom, clasped her hands together. "My son and my future son-in-law dressed for a wedding. If only they—"

"Mom." Hayley gave her mother a warning glance.

Kendra ducked her head to cover a smile. Everyone in town knew Virginia dreamed of Hayley and Abigail marrying Badger and Luke in a double ceremony, but neither couple was in a hurry to tie the knot.

Warren cleared his throat. "She was going to say *if only they'd remembered to polish their boots.*"

"Of course I was, Warren, darling."

Badger glanced down at his boots. "I would purely love to do it to please you, ma'am, but there's no point to it. They'll only be gettin' dusty again when we walk y'all down to the creek. Who's ready to go?"

Everyone was eager to see the setup. The guys took them in groups of four while Kendra remained at the house to greet new arrivals. She'd be the last person escorted down there and Badger had requested the honor of taking her. What a sweetie.

When the last of the guests were on their way to the creek, Kendra walked out on the porch. Ryker, Zane, Trevor and Badger had gathered in the front yard with Cody. Bryce had gone to the venue earlier since he was playing guitar, both as the guests arrived and during the processional.

Cody spotted her on the porch and climbed the steps to give her a kiss on the cheek. "What a great day, huh?"

Her throat tightened with love. "It's a spectacular day."

"I love you, Mom."

Fierce pride gripped her as she gazed up at her handsome son. Her baby. Her baby no more. "I love you, too, Cody."

"Hey, bridegroom!" Ryker called from the yard. "Time to get hitched, bro!"

"Can't wait!" He smiled and squeezed her shoulder before clattering down the steps to rejoin his brothers. They joked around with each other as they started down the path.

Badger turned and came up to the porch. "Ready, pretty lady?"

"I'm ready."

"Then let's get 'er done." He tucked her hand inside the crook of his arm as they started down the dirt path. "How're you holdin' up?"

She glanced at him and smiled. "I'm excited for Cody and Faith."

"Me, too." He gave her hand a squeeze. "They're gonna do great together."

"They are."

The faint chords of Bryce's guitar mingled with the chirp of birds in the pines. The music became more distinct with each step down the path. Nicole would join Bryce for a number during the ceremony. Faith and Cody hadn't wanted any other music.

Until now, Kendra had maintained an even keel. But the mellow thrum of Bryce's guitar was an emotional trigger. Better make conversation. "Are you working on your scratchboard project?" Yikes, but not about *that*.

"Yes, ma'am. But we don't have to talk about it if you'd rather not."

"No, no, I want to talk about it." *Too late to turn back, now.* "I think it's wonderful that you're branching out into something new. What're you starting with?"

"A portrait of that pup Delilah. One of these days Luke and Abigail will get hitched, and when they do, I'm givin' them something I didn't buy in a store."

"Great idea. I guess Virginia's still on her kick."

"You know, I'd be all for a double weddin'. But Hayley thinks we're not quite ready for that step. Luke and Abigail are still tryin' to figure out their livin' arrangement, so they're not ready, either. That said, it would be fun."

"It would." The sound of Bryce's guitar filled the air and she glimpsed the flash of white chairs through the trees. Then they stepped into the open. Oh, my. She gulped. Too beautiful for words.

The guys had put up a white lattice arch near the bank of the creek and decorated it with bright spring flowers. Sunlight flashed on the rippling water of the creek behind it, which added its music to Bryce's smooth melody. The guests had all dressed in festive colors that were perfectly framed by the white chairs.

And then...her boys. The joking had stopped and her strong, handsome sons stood with shoulders back and pride in every line of their bodies. She was the luckiest woman in the world.

"Like it?" Badger's deep voice was just what she needed to keep her from dissolving into a puddle of emotional goo.

"Love it." She took her seat in the front beside Jo. Deidre was in the next chair, with a vacant one reserved for Jim after he walked Faith down the aisle. Judy and Christine plus their husbands completed the row. Every one of them except Jim had known Cody since he was a baby.

Jo took her hand and held it tight as Bryce launched into the processional and the first bridesmaid started down the aisle closest to Kendra.

Once again, Mandy had outdone herself. For her fall wedding, she'd used autumn colors. For Faith's, she'd drawn from the pinks, blues, and yellows of the season. As she, Olivia, Nicole and April stood in all their ethereal beauty beside the flowered arch, Kendra counted her blessings. She'd given birth to sons, but now she had daughters, too.

At the back of the clearing, a horse nickered and Bryce launched into the wedding march. Everyone stood and turned as Jim led Faith in riding Ernie, who was wearing the saddle Faith had requested in place of a diamond engagement ring. Ernie's mane and tail were woven with more pink, blue and yellow ribbons than Kendra had ever seen on one horse.

Faith's gauzy, hopelessly romantic dress made her look like a wood nymph, especially with the crown of flowers she wore in place of a veil.

Walking over to Ernie, Cody embraced Jim. Then he reached up, lifted Faith from the saddle as if she were made of glass, and gently set her on her feet. Luke stepped in and led Ernie to the back of the clearing as Jim took his seat.

Warren smiled at the couple standing in front of him holding hands. The warmth of that smile said so much about the man. He clearly loved his job.

His gaze moved to the assembled guests. "I can't think of a more fitting place for these two beautiful souls to be united than under a Montana sky, surrounded by sunlight, rippling water and a gentle breeze."

Kendra gave up the fight. Tears dribbled down her cheeks as Warren continued, weaving in the traditional words of the ceremony with additions he, Faith and Cody had chosen during their sessions together.

Next to her, Jo sniffed. Then Deidre started. By the end of the ceremony, as Cody reverently kissed Faith, the women in the front row were a drippy mess. Jo came through with tissues for Kendra, herself and Deidre. Jim had to make use of his handkerchief for his own watering eyes.

And it was done. Everyone stood and applauded as Luke brought Ernie back down the aisle. Cody lifted Faith onto the saddle and swung up behind her. Turning the horse, he kicked Ernie into a trot. Once they cleared the chairs, Cody whipped off his hat, let out a whoop and the two of them cantered off as the guests cheered.

The groomsmen offered their arms to their respective sweethearts, waited for the dust to settle, and followed.

Jo glanced at Kendra, grinned and crooked her arm. "Let's go open us some wine, Gramma Ken."

"It'll be my pleasure, Gramma Jo." Arm in arm with her best friend, she marched down the path as they rehashed every minute of the ceremony.

"Two down, three to go," Jo said as they neared the house.

"That's only counting my biologic sons. I'm also excited about getting Badger, Luke and Michael married off. That's six more weddings we can look forward—" She stopped walking and stared at the parking area. "Jo."

Jo's arm tightened. "I see him."

"What the hell? Why would he…"

"Only one way to find out. Go ahead. Do your thing. I'll organize the troops."

Kendra's heart was beating way too fast. She was lightheaded, disoriented, unsure that she could make it all the way to the parking area. As she started toward it, Quinn came to meet her.

Out of breath, she stopped and waited, her hand to her chest. Had something terrible happened? Roxanne and Michael were here at the wedding. They were fine. Maybe Wes or Pete? But Quinn wouldn't come here if something was wrong with one of them.

His long strides brought him within three feet of her before he stopped, chest heaving, his gaze intense. "God, you look great."

"Th-thanks. Why are you—"

"I'm crashing the wedding party." He sucked in air. "I apologize for that. I just couldn't wait."

"For what?"

"I've...made a decision." He swallowed. "It concerns you."

"How?"

"I'm moving."

Her ears buzzed. "Where?"

"Here."

"To the ranch?"

"No, to Eagles Nest. I've put in an offer on the place across the road."

"You've..." She was so confused. "I don't...why would you..."

His smile was gentle. "Because I love you. Because it's no good me living up there and you living down here. One of us had to tackle that problem and so I will. I'm not asking to be your husband or your live-in lover. I just want to be...your neighbor. Your favorite neighbor."

She gasped for breath. "Can you do that?"

"I don't know, but I'll try my damnedest not to be a pest. You've made it clear you don't want your life to change, so I'll—"

"I mean can you move? What about your ranch?"

"As of today, it's up for sale."

"Quinn! You put your life's blood into that ranch. You can't just—"

"I can when it's the ranch or you. I choose you."

"Oh, my God." She put a trembling hand to her mouth. "You're serious."

"Dead serious." He came closer. "I can't live without you."

"I can't believe this."

He frowned. "Does that mean you don't like the idea?"

"No, I *love* the idea, I just can't—"

"That's all I need to hear." Swooping in, he took off his hat, wrapped her in his arms and captured her mouth.

That kiss was all it took. That wonderful, achingly familiar kiss. This was real. This was happening. She hadn't lost him forever. She hadn't lost him at all.

He lifted his head. "I know I can't keep this up. You have—"

"Gramma Jo's handling it. Kiss me some more."

"Gramma Jo? Is Mandy pregnant?"

"Don't know. But I do know one thing for sure."

"What's that?"

"I love you, Quinn Sawyer."

"So you said a week ago." He held her gaze. "You changed my life, sexy lady. And it's never changing back."

"I sure hope not, because you're going to make a fabulous neighbor." And she pulled him down for another kiss.

He was right. They couldn't keep doing this. But after the reception, after everyone had gone home, they could do this all night long.

Wes Sawyer faces an uphill climb wooing Ingrid Lindstrom after she swears off men in A COWBOY'S CHALLENGE, book ten in the McGavin Brothers series!

* * * * *

"Let me get the door." Wes fished out his key.

"It feels like it's been such a long time since the parade."

"Probably because we did a lot, today." He opened the door and motioned Ingrid inside. An overhead fixture in the entry and another in the upstairs hall lit the stairs as she began the climb, her footsteps on the wooden steps echoing in the silence.

He supposed they'd been alone in this building before, but it hadn't registered the way it did tonight. Abigail had held onto the front apartment even though she and Luke spent most of their time at his house adjacent to Wild Creek Ranch. Every so often they spent the night here, and he hadn't kept track of whether there was a routine to it.

For now, it was just Ingrid and him. And the poster on her wall. *A woman needs a man like a fish needs a bicycle.* He'd laughed at it this morning. After spending a wonderful day with her, he'd lost his sense of humor concerning that piece of art. He followed her up the stairs.

She waited for him at the top. Courtesy or something more? She gazed at him as he mounted the last couple of steps. "Thank you for inviting me to ride down to the park with you today." Her mouth tilted in a soft smile. "I had a really good time."

"So did I." He nudged back his hat and cleared his throat. "I just have to ask. What's that poster on your wall all about?"

Her smile faded.

Way to ruin the mood, idiot. "Never mind. Shouldn't have asked. It's none of my business."

"I wouldn't say that." She took a breath. "But if you don't mind, I'd rather not talk about it tonight."

"You don't have to talk about it, ever."

"I wondered if Roxanne might have—"

"No."

She nodded. "I should have known she wouldn't. She's a good friend."

Terrific. He'd just turned a sweet moment into an awkward one. "I should let you go, then. I'll...see you around." He started to turn away.

"Wait."

He glanced at her. Those gorgeous blue eyes had lost their sparkle, damn it. "Listen, I'm sorry. It's just that you seemed so happy to be with me today."

"I was. Today was special. And I'll explain about the poster. But it's...a long story, one better told another time." She stepped closer. "Goodnight, Wes." Without warning, she lifted to her toes and gave him a quick kiss on the mouth. Then she spun around and hurried down the hallway. Her door closed behind her with a soft click.

He stood where he was for a while, lips tingling from her drive-by kiss. What the hell did *that* mean?

New York Times bestselling author Vicki Lewis Thompson's love affair with cowboys started with the Lone Ranger, continued through Maverick, and took a turn south of the border with Zorro. She views cowboys as the Western version of knights in shining armor, rugged men who value honor, honesty and hard work. Fortunately for her, she lives in the Arizona desert, where broad-shouldered, lean-hipped cowboys abound. Blessed with such an abundance of inspiration, she only hopes that she can do them justice.

For more information about this prolific author, visit her website and sign up for her newsletter. She loves connecting with readers.

VickiLewisThompson.com

CPSIA information can be obtained
at www.ICGtesting.com
Printed in the USA
LVOW11s2316130618
580700LV00001B/110/P

9 781946 759450